Enid Blyton

FIVE-MINUTE STORIES

Look out for all of these enchanting story collections

by *Enid Blyton*

Enid Blyton

FIVE-MINUTE STORIES

Illustrations by Mark Beech

HODDER CHILDREN'S BOOKS

This collection first published in Great Britain in 2023
by Hodder & Stoughton

7 9 10 8

Enid Blyton® and Enid Blyton's signature are registered trade marks
of Hodder & Stoughton Limited
Text © 2023 Hodder & Stoughton Limited
Illustrations © 2023 Hodder & Stoughton Limited

A CIP catalogue record for this book is available from the British Library.

ISBN 978 1 444 96921 4

Typeset by Avon DataSet Ltd, Alcester, Warwickshire

Printed and bound in Great Britain by Clays Ltd, Elcograf S.p.A.

The paper and board used in this book are made from
wood from responsible sources.

MIX
Paper from
responsible sources
FSC® C104740

Hodder Children's Books
An imprint of Hachette Children's Group
Part of Hodder & Stoughton
Carmelite House
50 Victoria Embankment
London EC4Y 0DZ

An Hachette UK Company
www.hachette.co.uk
www.hachettechildrens.co.uk

Contents

Eight Times Nine!

Eight Times Nine!

'EIGHT TIMES nine! Eight times nine! It won't come right. I've tried and I've tried!'

Bill heard the cross voice as he came through Breezy Wood and stopped. What a funny thing to say in the middle of the wood! Eight times nine! Well, *he* knew what they were, because he knew all his tables! Bill peered round a tree to see who was talking.

'Eight times nine! Sixty-three! No, I've tried that and it's wrong!' It was a little whiskery man who was speaking, as he bent over something on the ground. He looked extraordinarily like a magical brownie, but Bill was sure he couldn't be. Nobody saw magical brownies nowadays.

'Eight times *nine*!' said the little fellow and began to arrange something here and there. Bill stared in surprise. He had a large number of fir cones on the ground before him, set out in three lines. Nearby was a small heap of acorns and beside these were about a dozen chestnuts.

What *could* he be doing? Bill peered further round the tree, wondering if he should ask the little man. Then, without even turning round, the fellow spoke to him.

'I can see you peeping round that tree. You needn't peep. Come right out.'

'How did you see me?' said Bill, surprised, coming out from behind the tree trunk. 'You weren't even looking at me.'

'I've got eyes in the back of my head,' said the little man, and Bill had quite a shock when he suddenly saw two eyes looking at him through holes in the back of the man's pointed cap. 'Haven't you ever heard of eyes like that? I've got them in the front too, of course!' He turned and looked at Bill.

Yes, certainly he had eyes there too, bright green and twinkling. And his two pointed ears were green as well! Then he frowned. 'It's a pity you interrupted me,' he said. 'I'm in the middle of a spell – but this eight times nine must be wrong. I cannot make the spell work.'

'Oh – are you making a spell?' said Bill, and suddenly felt excited. 'Can I help you?'

'I don't know. Do you know your tables?' asked the little fellow. He was most certainly a magical brownie, for his whiskers fell almost to his feet.

'Yes, of course,' said Bill. 'We learn them at school. Didn't you?'

'No. Magical brownies didn't go to school when I was young,' said the little fellow. 'Now look, the first bit of the spell is: *Fir cones, eight nines, set out in three lines*. Well, *I* can't seem to make them come right. But the next bit is easy: *Acorns, two threes, thrown up in the breeze*. Well, two threes are six, aren't they?'

'Yes, that's right,' said Bill, looking at the six acorns in a little pile. 'What about those chestnuts?'

'*Chestnuts – six twos, set all round my shoes*,' said the magical brownie. 'Are six twos twelve? Have I got enough?'

'Yes,' said Bill, counting the chestnuts. 'Well, it's only the fir cones that must be wrong, if your spell won't work. If you want eight nines of those, you ought to have seventy-two.'

'I thought eight nines were sixty-three,' said the magical brownie, and frowned again. 'I haven't enough then. Are you quite sure seventy-two is right, because sometimes when a spell goes wrong, nasty things happen?'

'Did anything happen when you tried to make the spell with sixty-three fir cones then, instead of seventy-two?' asked Bill.

'Good gracious, yes. My ears turned green – haven't you noticed?' said the magical brownie. Bill nodded, rather startled. What an awful thing to happen!

'Well, I'd better take your word for it that eight times nine are seventy-two,' said the magical brownie. 'But mind you, if anything horrid happens – fingers growing out of my nose, or something like that – I shall know you've told me wrong.'

'You can easily prove I'm right,' said Bill. 'Get some more fir cones to make yours up to seventy-two, then set them out in nines, and if you have eight rows of nine, you'll be safe!'

Well, that's what the magical brownie did, with Bill's help. He fetched more fir cones, then set them out in rows of nine – and there were eight rows, of course! He counted them and they made seventy-two. Good! 'Now I've got to make only *three* rows of the fir cones, boy. That won't be easy!'

'Good gracious – of course it will!' said Bill. 'You want twenty-four in each row.' And sure enough, he was right, of course. (Did *you* know he was?)

Then the spell began. There were the seventy-two fir cones set out in three lines. There were the six acorns in a pile. And there were the twelve chestnuts set neatly all round the magical brownie's shoes. He began to sing where he stood:

> '*Fir cones, eight nines,*
> *Set out in three lines,*
> *Acorns, two threes,*
> *Thrown up in the breeze!*
> *Chestnuts, six twos,*
> *Set all round my shoes!*
> *Then whistle and sing,*
> *Dance round in a ring,*
> *And maybe for you,*
> *A wish will come true!*'

When he had sung the last four lines, the little fellow suddenly threw the acorns into the air, then whistled loudly, and began to sing, dancing round madly in a ring all the time. As he danced Bill heard a sudden clinking, jingling noise.

The magical brownie stopped all at once and grinned at Bill. 'My wish came true that time,' he said, and he put his hands into his pockets and brought out dozens of tiny gold pieces that fell to the ground and glittered brightly.

'Money!' he said. 'I'm a hundred years old tomorrow and I badly wanted to give a party, but I couldn't afford to. Now I've got plenty of money because my wish came true. I'm glad you came along. Here's a little of my money for you!'

And he pressed a few of the tiny gold pieces into Bill's hand. Then he skipped away through the trees and was lost to sight.

Bill stared at the money – magical brownie money! Was it worth anything? Could he buy something with it? He began to run through the wood, clutching it in his hand, excited. Fancy having

9

magical-brownie money to spend!

But nobody would take it. The shopkeepers laughed at him. '*That's* not money! You know it isn't. Whoever saw money as small as that!'

Bill was very disappointed. But soon he cheered up. Could he remember the spell? *Could* he? Suppose he could remember it all and make a wish for himself!

But suppose he *couldn't* remember it very well and something went wrong! Dare he risk it? He didn't want *his* ears suddenly to turn green, or fingers to grow out of his nose! He didn't really want eyes at the back of his head either.

So now he is writing down the spell he heard the magical brownie sing. Do you suppose he'll remember it perfectly. Well – could *you*? Write it down now and see!

(*But don't look back to see what it was!*)

The Mouse in the
Window

The Mouse in the Window

EVERY MORNING on her way to school, Dinah stopped to look in at the toy-shop window. The dolls sat at the back, with an enormous teddy bear, two toy soldiers and a panda on each side of them. A toy fort stood in the middle, and a doll's house at the side. Other toys lay here and there, and it really took a long time to see each one.

Dinah was one of a big family of nine children, and had only one toy of her own – a small doll with a broken arm and very little hair. The doll had no clothes except for a dirty, torn frock, but Dinah loved her very much, and always took her to bed with her.

'One day, when I'm rich, I'll buy you a new frock!' she told her doll. 'And I'll get your arm mended. The others laugh at you, Rosebud, but I never will!'

Dinah thought the dolls in the toy shop were wonderful – so very, very grand! She loved the big doll's house too, with its front door just ajar, and its windows partly open, showing the tiny curtains behind. And she thought that one of the very nicest things was the toy sweet shop, with its tiny scales for weighing, and its little bottles of real sweets.

There was very little money to spare for buying toys for nine children, even on birthdays! So Dinah feasted her eyes on the toys in the window instead.

All the children loved the toy shop, and the little woman who kept it smiled when she saw them peeping in at the window. But lately she hadn't smiled at all.

It was really Peter who began the trouble. He didn't want only to see the toys in the window – he wanted to see all those in the shop too. So he went in and fingered the soldiers and stood them up, and got into the small pedal car and rode it round the shop.

'What do you want to buy?' asked Mrs Brown, the toy-shop woman, after Peter had been there for twenty minutes, fingering everything.

'Oh, nothing,' said Peter. 'I just want to see what you've got.'

He brought his friends to roam round the little toy shop too, and soon one or two things were broken – a small petrol pump from the toy garage and a little wooden chair belonging to a doll's house set.

'Now this won't do,' said Mrs Brown. 'Unless you want to buy something, you mustn't come into the shop. I'll have nothing left soon!'

Peter was cross. He was also very sly and artful. He went in with sixpence and asked Mrs Brown if she had any marbles. He knew they were kept on the back shelf. She went up the ladder slowly, her back turned to Peter – and the naughty boy picked up two tiny cars and put them into his pocket.

He looked at the marbles and bought two. Then

out he went, pleased to think he had something for nothing in his pocket. After that he sent John in, and John did the same thing when Mrs Brown was going up the ladder.

It was then that the old lady lost her welcoming smile for the children, and looked at them crossly when they came in. Were they going to steal from her again? Could she trust *any* of them? The nice children, who would never dream of stealing, couldn't think why she had changed, and they grew afraid of her.

Dinah had hardly ever been into the shop. She just stared and stared into the window, wondering if she would *ever* have a doll's house like the one she saw there, or a tea set like the one in the corner.

One day, on her way to school, she stopped as usual and looked into the window – and she suddenly saw a very peculiar thing. Somebody looked out of the top window of the doll's house!

Dinah jumped and blinked. When she looked again, there was nobody there. 'It looked like a mouse!'

said Dinah to herself. 'A dear little mouse with a woffly kind of nose.'

She had heard the tale of Mary Mouse who lived in a doll's house and kept it clean – but Mary Mouse was brown and this little mouse looked pale-coloured. She looked and looked to see if she could spy it again, but she couldn't.

It must have been a mistake, she thought. *I must have imagined it!* She went off to school at a run, for she was late.

When she ran home for dinner, she stopped at the toy-shop window again and looked at the doll's house. And there, peeping out of the front door, was the little pointed nose again, with big whiskers on each side of it, and two bright eyes behind.

'It *is* a mouse – a *white* mouse!' said Dinah to herself. 'It's living in that doll's house. It just waits for me to come by and then it peeps out at me. It's my secret. I shan't tell anybody at all!'

Well, every day for a week Dinah stopped to look

at the mouse. Once she didn't see it at all – but usually she saw it somewhere in the doll's house, and once it was cuddled up against a doll. It really was a dear little thing. Sometimes it was difficult for even Dinah's sharp eyes to see it, because it was quite clever at hiding when people pressed their noses against the window.

And then one day after a week had gone by, Dinah saw the mouse in the sweet shop! It had gnawed through the tiny corks in the sweet bottles, and it was eating the little sweets inside!

'Oh, dear – you shouldn't do that!' said Dinah. 'Nobody will buy that dear little sweet shop if you nibble all the sweets, White Mouse.'

But the mouse just looked at her with bright eyes and went on nibbling. Then someone else came by whistling, and he scurried into the doll's house through the front door.

Next day Dinah looked for him again – and she saw him at the back of the shop, pulling something white out of a cuddly doll's leg! Good gracious – he had nibbled a hole in the doll's soft leg, and was pulling out all the cotton wool that stuffed her to make her soft and cuddly!

That was too much! Really, Dinah couldn't allow even a nice little white mouse to steal sweets and spoil the lovely dolls! So she went into the little toy shop.

'Oh, Mrs Brown,' she said, 'did you know that a mouse lives in the doll's house in the window?'

'Now don't you come telling me silly tales like that!' said Mrs Brown. 'My old cat hunts mice – he'd never let one run about my toy shop. As for a mouse living in a doll's house, that's nonsense!'

'But, Mrs Brown – you just go to the back of your window, and open the doll's house door and look inside,' said Dinah.

'Aha! And what will *you* do while my back is turned?' said Mrs Brown. 'I know these little tricks that you children play on me now. You get me to turn my back – and then you put something into your pockets!

I'm ashamed of you – coming along with a tale like this just to make me turn my back for a moment!'

Dinah stared at the old lady in surprise. 'But – it's not just a tale,' she said. 'And I wouldn't *ever* take anything from your shop. I'm telling you the truth.'

'Now you run away,' said Mrs Brown. 'And don't come back and tell me there's a monkey in the window next, for I shan't believe you! Run away!'

Dinah went off, blinking away tears. She met her big brother as she ran home, and he went up to her at once. 'What's the matter, Dinah? What are you crying for?'

'Oh – it's about a little white mouse,' said Dinah. 'But it's a secret.'

'A white mouse! Where is it? Donald's lost his very best one,' said big Bill. 'It might be his.'

Donald was Bill's friend. He was the son of the village policeman, and he bred white mice and rats.

'Oh!' said Dinah. 'Yes, it might be Donald's. I never thought of that. Let's go and ask him.'

So they went to call on Donald. 'Have you lost a very pretty fat little white mouse?' asked Dinah.

'Yes. About ten days ago,' said Donald. 'I carried her about in my pocket, and she must have escaped – because when I got home my pocket was empty. She was my best mouse too, my very best. Why – have you found a white mouse?'

'Not exactly,' said Dinah. 'But I know where one is – in the toy-shop window! And it lives in the doll's house there, and eats the sweets out of the toy sweet shop – and now it's pulling cotton wool out of the leg of one of the dolls.'

'Goodness! Why ever didn't you go and tell old Mrs Brown?' said Donald.

'I did,' said Dinah, 'and she was horrid to me. She said that I'd come to play a trick on her, like some of the other children do – make her turn her back to look for something and then pocket a toy when she's not looking. As if I'd be a thief!'

She began to cry again. Big Bill petted her. 'Don't

cry, Di. Poor Mrs Brown does have a hard time now, with some of the children in the village. But Donald here will tell his father, and he'll soon put it about that any boy or girl playing tricks on Mrs Brown will be punished. What's the good of having a policeman if he can't keep the children in order?'

'Let's go to the toy shop now,' said Donald. 'I'd like my mouse back. If she's pulling cotton wool out of that doll's leg, it means that she's going to build a nest, and put some young ones there. I don't want to lose a whole family!'

So they all three went off to Mrs Brown's. She smiled at Donald, because she knew his father, the village policeman, very well. 'And what have *you* come for?' she said.

'To get my white mouse,' said Donald, much to her astonishment. 'I came in here about ten days ago, Mrs Brown, to buy a doll for my sister, do you remember? Well, I had this white mouse in my pocket, and it must have escaped when I was here – because Dinah says it's in your window, living in the doll's house there!'

'Well I never!' said Mrs Brown, looking down at Dinah. 'So her story was true, bless her – and I was so cross and unkind, wasn't I, Dinah? I sent her away!'

'The mouse is in the window now, Mrs Brown,' said Dinah. 'Come and see.'

They all went out into the street and looked in at the window – and the tiny mouse peeped out of one of the top windows of the doll's house! Donald gave a little cry.

'Yes – that's my mouse. Well, well – to think she set up house here, in your window, Mrs Brown. May I catch her, please?'

'Oh, yes, Donald,' said Mrs Brown. 'The little scamp – eating my sweets, and nibbling my dolls! I'm sorry I didn't believe Dinah's tale – but, you know, so many children are mean to me now, and take this and that when I'm not looking.'

'I'll see that that is stopped, Mrs Brown,' said Donald. 'My father will visit the school and give a stern warning about it. You needn't be afraid again.'

'Oh, thank you, Donald,' said Mrs Brown. The boy went back into the shop, and put his head into the window. He made a soft little noise, and the mouse heard it at once. She knew who made it too! She ran out of the doll's house joyfully, raced up Donald's sleeve and disappeared.

Donald opened the front of the doll's house. In one of the doll's beds there was piled a heap of cotton wool, and six tiny baby white mice lay there, their noses in their paws!

'I thought so!' said Donald, pleased. 'Well, now I've got a whole family, instead of just one mouse. Thank you, Dinah – it's all because of you! Would you like one of these mice?'

'No, thank you,' said Dinah. 'We've already got a pet cat.'

'Well, let me buy you a doll?' said Donald. But again Dinah shook her head.

'No, thank you. I've one of my own, and I don't want another.'

'Dinah – she's an *awful* doll,' said Bill. 'Her arm's broken and she's got hardly any hair. She's a scarecrow doll!'

'She's *not*!' said Dinah fiercely.

'Well, listen – I'll get her arm mended for you,' said Donald. 'Will you let me do that? Mrs Brown will send her to the doll's hospital and get it mended. Won't you, Mrs Brown?'

'Indeed I will,' said Mrs Brown, smiling. 'You bring her in, Dinah.'

So next day Dinah took Rosebud to the toy shop and gave her to Mrs Brown. 'I'm going to make your doll some new clothes,' said the old lady. 'Just to show I'm sorry for being cross with you. Come back for her in a week.'

So Dinah went back in a week. Sitting on the counter was the prettiest little doll she had ever seen – a doll with a mass of golden curls, and dressed in a blue silk frock with a white sash tied round her waist.

Dinah looked at her – was it Rosebud – no, it

couldn't be. But it was! She had new hair, a new arm, she was clean – and she was wearing a whole set of new clothes, even a little vest underneath, and shoes and stockings!

'Do you like her?' said Mrs Brown. 'She's your old Rosebud. Feel her.'

Dinah took the doll into her arms, and beamed at Mrs Brown at once. 'Yes, she's Rosebud. I'd know the feel of her anywhere. Oh, *thank* you, Mrs Brown. You *are* kind!'

'Donald bought the new arm and new hair,' said Mrs Brown. 'I just made the clothes. Well, well – I'll certainly listen to you next time you come with a strange tale – yes, even if you tell me there are live kangaroos and lions and tigers jumping about in the Noah's Ark!'

Dinah still looks carefully into the toy-shop window when she passes by, but I don't suppose she'll see anything *quite* so exciting as a mouse in the doll's house again!

What! No Cheese?

What! No Cheese?

THERE WAS once a little bird who loved cheese. He thought it was far, far nicer than butter, and if he could steal some, he would!

He flew into the grocer's shop and pecked a big hole in the cheese there.

He sat on Dame Tippy's shopping basket as she went home and pecked a big piece out of her bit of cheese too.

And do you know, he even went into Old Man Dingle's garden and pecked the tiny bits of cheese out of the mouse traps set there to catch mice who ate the peas! Wasn't he a thief?

He ate so much cheese that he grew quite yellow, and people began to call him the cheese-bird.

They thought he was a greedy little thing, and if ever he came to tea with them they made sure not to have any cheese, for if they did he would eat up every scrap.

So when he popped into their houses and they offered him bread and butter, or bread and jam, he would put his head on one side, look down his beak in a very haughty manner, and say, 'What! No cheese?'

He went to tea with Dame Frilly, and she gave him egg sandwiches. 'What! No cheese?' he cried, and wouldn't eat a thing.

He went to supper with Dickory-Dock, who had a nice meal of sardines and cocoa ready.

'What! No cheese?' cried the greedy bird, and he wouldn't touch anything at all.

It seemed such a waste of a meal, because Dickory-Dock couldn't possibly eat it all himself.

One day the pixie Long-Legs gave a fine party.

There were strawberries and cream, vanilla ices and lemonade, and you would have thought anyone would have been pleased, wouldn't you?

But the little yellow bird turned up his beak at everything. 'What! No cheese?' he cried again.

Long-Legs was angry. 'No,' she said, 'there isn't any cheese, you greedy little bird. Who stole cheese from the grocer? Who stole Old Man Dingle's mouse trap cheese? Go away, you greedy thing, and don't come back here again! Sing a song about cheese if you want to – *we* shan't listen.'

So the little bird had to fly away into our world. There he found that people were as kind as could be and put out crumbs and potato and coconut and fat – but, of course, not a scrap of cheese!

And so all day long he sits on the telegraph wires, or on a high hedge, and sings the same little song over and over again. 'Little bit of bread and no cheese! Little bit of bread and no cheese! Little bit of bread and no cheese!'

Have you heard him? He is singing it this summer just as usual for I've heard him three times already today.

We call him the yellowhammer and he is a bird rather like a sparrow, but yellow ... and how he sings the little song: 'Little bit of bread and no cheese!' Do see if you can hear him. He sings it as plainly as anything.

The Two Boys

The Two Boys

ONCE UPON a time there were two boys who lived in the same village. One was called Jim and the other John. They were both tall, strong boys, the cleverest boys in their school. When the time came for them to leave, their teacher looked about for a good job for them. He soon heard of one in the next town.

'I have heard of an excellent job in the town,' he told them. 'The master of the big works there wants an office boy. Now one of you should get that job, for it may lead to a fine future, if you work hard and do your best. Tomorrow you must each go to see the master of the works, and he will choose between you. Jim, you be there at ten, and you, John, at eleven.'

'Thank you, sir,' said the boys, and went running home to tell their parents of the job they might get.

Now, the way to the town was across the countryside, over the hills and by way of a shallow stream that could easily be waded through at a certain part, for the water there was barely ankle-deep. There were no buses, for the little village was too small to be bothered about. The boys knew the way well. They both laid out their best suits that night and cleaned their boots till they shone.

In the night there came a terrible storm. The thunder rolled, the lightning flashed and the rain poured down by the bucketful. The little stream swelled into a torrent, and great boulders fell down the hillside on to the path that led to the town.

At nine o'clock Jim set out to walk to the town. The storm was over, the sky was clear. When he came near the stream the boy stopped in dismay. Great rocks hid the path and the stream was too deep to wade. He would get his new suit wet! So he turned back and went home. *It is impossible to get to town today*, he thought.

At ten o'clock John set out, also in his new suit, and with his shoes shining like glass. When he saw the great stones on the path, and the swollen stream rushing by, he, like Jim, stopped in dismay. But he did not go back home. He stood and thought for a while, and then his face brightened.

I can clear a path all right, he thought, *for I am strong enough to lift these stones – and if I throw them into the stream I can use them as stepping-stones across and I shall not need to get my suit wet! I can take off my boots and stockings!*

The boy worked hard. He lifted the stones and staggered with them to the stream. He threw them in, and soon he had made a pathway of stones across the rushing stream!

It's a fine thing to make obstacles into stepping-stones! thought the boy. *I shall get to town all right!*

And so he did, though he had to run all the rest of the way to get there in time. He got the job, of course, because Jim hadn't arrived.

That is ten years ago. Now John is head of the works in the town – and Jim goes to him whenever he needs a job! 'I might be where you are, John,' Jim often says, 'if only *I'd* made obstacles into stepping-stones too!'

Sally's Stitch

SALLY WAS a little girl who was always laughing, so you can guess she was rather nice. I do like people who laugh, don't you? Well, you would have liked Sally very much. Everybody did.

One day she went for a walk across the fields. She went quietly, for the grass was thick and soft. And quite suddenly she came across five or six pixies playing the most surprising games. Sally knew they were pixies because she had seen pictures of them in books, just as you have. She was simply delighted. She sat down behind a bush and watched.

'I can stand on my head on the gatepost!' cried a

small pixie – and he did. It was really funny to see him.

'I can curl myself up into a ball and roll along!' cried another. And he curled himself up, arms and legs and all, and began to roll over and over just like a ball. All the pixies laughed to see him.

'Can you bounce yourself, can you bounce yourself?' squealed a pixie nearby. 'Oh, do try!'

'Of course I can!' cried the ball-pixie, and he threw himself up into the air. 'Look out – I'm going to bounce!'

And he bounced. Goodness, how he bounced! Just as if he were a big rubber ball. Up into the air he went, and down he came again. He bounced on to a prickly thistle, gave a loud yell and bounced high again.

Sally began to laugh. She couldn't help it. She laughed till the tears came into her eyes. Then she got a stitch in her side from laughing, and that made her feel very uncomfortable. 'Oh, dear,' she said, 'oh, dear!' And she put her hand against her side to try and ease the stitch there. You know how funny you feel when you get a stitch in your side from running or laughing, don't you?

The pixies heard Sally's laughter. It was a nice sound. They ran round the bush to see who was there. And they found Sally, laughing away, with her hand pressed to her side.

'What's the matter?' they cried anxiously. 'Why do you hold yourself there? Are you hurt?'

'Oh, I've got such a big stitch in my side!' said Sally. 'I can't get rid of it. Oh, it hurts me! I can't breathe properly. I can't walk with it either.'

'Poor little girl!' cried a big pixie. 'Who put the stitch there? Did you sew it there yourself? Was the needle sharp?'

'Of course not,' said Sally, beginning to giggle again. 'Don't be so silly.'

'Poor child!' said the pixies, looking at Sally out of their green eyes. 'She's got a stitch in her side. Somebody has stitched her up so that she can't walk properly. Poor child.'

'Oh, don't make me laugh again or my stitch will

get worse!' cried Sally. 'Oh, dear – it's the worst stitch I've ever had. But really, you did look so funny when you bounced on that thistle, pixie. Oh, my – I shall start laughing again if I'm not careful!'

She tried to walk a few steps, but she couldn't because of the stitch in her side. The pixies felt really sorry for her. They talked among themselves.

'Let's call Dame Snippit. She can take out the stitch. The poor girl will never get home. What a shame that somebody has stitched her up like that.'

'Dame Snippit! Dame Snippit!' called a pixie loudly. 'Are you anywhere about? You're wanted.'

To Sally's enormous surprise, a neat little door opened in a nearby oak tree and out stepped a dame, with her hair in ringlets, and scissors and tape measures all hung about her waist.

'What's the matter?' she asked.

'This poor child has got a stitch in her side, so she can't walk,' explained a pixie. 'Can you take out the stitch?'

'I could snip it,' said Dame Snippit, taking up her largest pair of scissors. 'That's the quickest way of taking out a stitch, you know.'

'Oh, I don't want it snipped,' said Sally in alarm. 'It's not that kind of stitch, really it isn't.'

'Well, what sort of a stitch is it then, my dear?' asked Dame Snippit in surprise.

'Well, it's a laughing-stitch,' said Sally.

'Never heard of one,' said Dame Snippit. 'Come, come – let me snip it for you, then you can walk. You shouldn't let people put a stitch in your side like that. Very silly of you.'

'I didn't, I didn't,' said Sally, and she tried to run away. But the stitch in her side caught her and she had to stop. She saw Dame Snippit take up her scissors again.

Then Sally remembered that her mother had always said she could get rid of a stitch in her side by bending over and touching her toes with her fingers.

I'd better try that before Dame Snippit does anything

stupid! thought the little girl. So she bent herself right over and touched her toes. When she stood up straight again, lo and behold! Her stitch was quite gone! Hurray!

'The stitch is gone!' she cried. 'It's all right, pixie, it's all right, Dame Snippit. The stitch is gone.'

'I suppose you broke it when you bent over,' said Dame Snippit in astonishment. 'Well, well – don't you go having stitches inside you any more. Most uncomfortable, I call it.'

Sally said goodbye and ran home. On the way she remembered again how the pixie had bounced himself on the prickly thistle, and she stopped and began to laugh.

And she got another stitch in her side! But she didn't say a word about it. No – she wasn't going to have Dame Snippit trying to snip the stitch with her big scissors!

Do you ever get a stitch? Well, try Sally's way of curing it, and see if it goes!

The Brown Rat and the Wren

The Brown Rat and
the Wren

ONCE UPON a time the little wren saw the lean brown rat running by, and he sent a loud song after him.

'The lean brown rat is running there,
Beware, you birds and beasts, beware.
He has a fierce and angry glare,
Beware! Beware! Beware!'

The last words the wren sang so loudly and shrilly that all the blackbirds nearby set up their alarm cries, and the sparrows flew to the topmost branches of the trees, chirruping in fright. The little mice scurried down their holes, trembling, and the grey squirrel shot up his tree.

The lean brown rat was angry. He glared up at the stumpy-tailed wren. 'There is nothing I like better than wren's eggs!' he said. 'Wait till you build a nest and your mate lays eggs! I will watch for them – and eat them up!'

He ran off into the hedge. The wren stared after him with bright black eyes. So the rat was going to watch for his nest and eat the eggs, was he? The wren was afraid. He knew how cunning and how cruel the rat was – the cleverest creature in the whole countryside. The tiny bird hunched his head into his shoulders and thought hard.

Presently he flew off, singing shrilly. He had the loudest voice for his size of any bird round about. He flew to the hayrick and looked about for a nice place to nest. He already had a mate. She came to help him. There was a lot of whispering between them, and then the cock began to make a hole for a nest.

THE BROWN RAT AND THE WREN

The brown rat ran out from beneath the rick and watched. *Good!* he thought. *I know where the nest is!*

But although the cock made a nest there, he did not line it! No – it was just a nest to catch the rat's eye. He did not mean to let his mate lay eggs there! After he had made a nice little nest, he flew off to the other side of the rick. He made a nest there too!

'If the rat finds the other nest, we will lay our eggs in this one,' he said. 'We will wait!'

The rat watched the first nest and waited impatiently for the eggs. But by chance he discovered the other nest, and the wrens saw him peeping inside it one morning.

'This won't do!' said the wren. 'We will build a third nest – and a fourth nest – yes, and even a fifth nest if need be! The one that the rat does not find we will line carefully and have for our eggs!'

So the wrens made six nests altogether – three in the rick, one in the thatched roof of a shed and two in the thatch of a cottage. The rat found them all but the one in the shed. This one the wrens lined and the little Jenny wren laid five dear little eggs there.

The rat was angry. There were no eggs in the nests he had found. 'You are playing tricks on me!' he snickered to the wrens. 'I'm not going to hunt for any more empty nests!'

He disappeared, and went to live down at the bottom of the lane.

The wrens were glad. They sat on the eggs happily, and hatched them out into tiny birds, all of whom sang the same loud song whenever they saw the lean brown rat gliding by! And to this day the wrens sing this loud, defiant song, with the shrill 'Beware! Beware! Beware!' at the end. And before they choose a nest they make half a dozen first – just in case the brown rat is up to his tricks once more!

Keep Your Eyes Open!

THIS IS the story of a small boy who kept his eyes open. His name was Bobby, and he went to school every day, just as you do. He had rather an exciting way to go to school, because most of the road he had to walk ran beside the railway line. So Bobby knew all about signals and trains and lines.

There was a level crossing not far off too, though Bobby didn't have to go over this. When the train was due to come along, old Mrs Lewis, who lived in the little cottage beside the crossing, swung the big gates open for the train – and that meant no one could cross and get run over. When the train had gone, Mrs Lewis swung the gates back again, so that anyone could walk over the line.

Every day when Bobby went home from school he noticed a great many things. He always saw what flowers were out in the gardens; he noticed the new cart that the baker had; he saw the hole where a small mouse lived in a green bank. He saw the starlings sitting on the roofs, and he even noticed which chimneys were smoking and which weren't! He always knew which way the wind was by watching the smoke from Mrs Lewis's chimney. If it streamed across the line, the wind was in the west. If it went the other way, it was blowing from the east. Up and down the line meant the wind was in the north or south.

One morning when Bobby came home from school he looked as usual for the smoke from Mrs Lewis's chimney – but to his surprise there was none!

Now perhaps another boy might not have thought anything about this at all – but Bobby was the kind that always kept his eyes and ears and mind wide open! So he began to think.

Mrs Lewis always has a fire to cook with. If she has a fire, there is smoke – but there isn't smoke, so she can't have a fire. If there isn't a fire, she can't cook her dinner. Why doesn't she want any dinner?

He thought about it, and decided to go and knock at her door to see what she was having for dinner. He was very friendly with the old lady, and often took her old newspapers to read. So he left the road, and ran down the lane that led to the level crossing. He knocked at Mrs Lewis's door. A voice told him to come in. So in he went.

And what do you think? The poor old woman had slipped and broken her leg that morning! So her fire had gone out – because she couldn't even get up from the floor!

'Bobby! Open the level-crossing gates quickly!' said Mrs Lewis. 'The train is due in one minute. It will smash the gates to pieces, and there might be a dreadful accident!'

Bobby rushed outside. He could see the train far away in the distance, tearing down the line. He swung the first gate open. He ran across and swung back the other one. It clicked into place just as the train tore past – in safety! How Bobby's heart beat!

He ran back and got Mrs Lewis on to the sofa. Then off he went for the doctor, and for the old woman's son. And do you know, by the time the afternoon came, and the story had gone round the town, Bobby found himself quite a hero!

'Please don't make a fuss!' he said. 'I only kept my eyes open, and saw there was no smoke from Mrs Lewis's chimney!'

Keep your eyes open too, boys and girls – you never know when you might get a chance like Bobby!

Up the Chimney!

Up the Chimney!

'GO AND get your hats and coats on and we will set off to the games field!' called Miss Brown. 'Quick, now, because we are late.'

The children ran to the cloakroom to get their things. They all wore navy blue berets, and navy blue coats with the red school badge on. What a scramble there was in the cloakroom!

'Where's my coat? You're treading on it, Michael. Get off it at once!'

'My beret, my beret, has anyone seen it? It's not on my peg. Blow!'

One by one the children ran out of the cloakroom

to the hall, where Miss Brown was waiting for them. Late-comers were left behind to do lessons, so everyone was as quick as could be!

Monica couldn't find her beret. She hunted everywhere for it. *Where* was it? Miss Brown wouldn't take her if she hadn't got it. Whatever had happened to it?

She looked at all the pegs there. Every one of them was empty – except for one. That was Eileen's. She had a bad leg and was not allowed to play games that week, so she had stayed behind in the classroom to read. On her peg hung her coat and her beret.

Monica looked round and saw that the cloakroom was empty. Nobody was there to see her snatch Eileen's beret from the peg and cram it on her own head! The children were not allowed to wear each other's berets, Monica knew that – but she wasn't going to miss games. She would wear Eileen's, and nobody would know.

She ran to join the others. 'I was *just* going without you, Monica,' said Miss Brown impatiently. 'Come along, everyone.'

Off they went to the sports field, which was a little way away. There was a small pavilion there, and the children hung up their things. Monica was careful to slip Eileen's beret into the pocket of her coat. She didn't want anyone to notice that it had Eileen's name inside and not hers!

They had a fine game and came back to get their clothes. Monica put on her coat and was just going to put on Eileen's beret when Jack snatched it from her and threw it up to the ceiling. Soon all the children were snatching each other's berets and flinging them about. It was a silly game they played when they were excited.

Monica snatched Eileen's beret as it fell – but Harry grabbed it and sent it flying again. It caught on a nail, and as Monica reached up for it and gave it a tug, the nail tore the school badge half off the beret.

Blow! It hung all sideways. Miss Brown would be sure to notice it.

'Here she is! Here's Miss Brown!' the whisper went round, and immediately the hat-throwing stopped and fourteen perfectly good children went out to join Miss Brown.

By the time that Monica had got back to school, the badge on the beret she wore was hanging by a thread. She must mend it before she put it back on Eileen's peg. How could she manage to do that without being seen? Perhaps she could do it in the dinner hour. She always stayed to dinner at school, and there was usually half an hour afterwards to spend as she liked.

Eileen stayed to dinner too, so that was all right. She wouldn't miss her beret. Monica stuffed it into the pocket of her coat again, when she hung it up in the cloakroom.

After dinner she thought of the beret again. Now, could she manage to sew on that badge without anyone seeing her? If Miss Brown knew she had taken Eileen's beret to wear, she would be cross – and it had Eileen's name in it, so that anyone might see it.

She went out of the dining hall as soon as she had finished her dinner. She must go to the sewing room and get a workbasket there. The big children were allowed to have their own baskets, so there would be plenty. She only wanted a reel of blue cotton and a needle.

She slipped into the sewing room. She knew where the little workbaskets were kept – in the big cupboard. She opened the door and looked inside. She took the first basket she saw – a pretty little round one. She didn't know whose it was. She took it to a desk and threaded a needle with navy blue cotton. She hunted for a thimble but there wasn't one in the basket. She went back to the cupboard and found one in another basket – a lovely little silver one.

She sat down in a chair and began to sew on the badge. Soon she wanted scissors and saw a pair on the teacher's desk. She began to snip a few frayed bits off the badge. And then suddenly she heard someone coming!

She leapt up with the beret and the workbasket, putting the scissors into it hurriedly. Where could she hide everything? Nobody was allowed to take a workbasket from the cupboard except in sewing lesson!

Monica didn't dare to slip the beret and the basket into a desk. Someone might open it that very afternoon! She saw a big wastepaper basket stuffed half full of paper standing in the corner. She ran to it, lifted up the paper and stuffed everything underneath. Then she rammed the paper back again and ran to the windowsill just as the door opened.

Rita came in to put out the sewing things for the afternoon's lesson. She was surprised to see Monica there. 'I'm just seeing to the flowers,' said Monica hurriedly. 'Some of them want water.'

'Carry on then,' said Rita. 'I've only come to find all the sewing things for Miss Faber.'

Monica got some water and began to fill up the vases. She began to worry about the wastepaper basket. The school caretaker collected all the baskets after afternoon school, and emptied them into an enormous dustbin. He might empty this one – and the beret and the workbasket would be thrown away as rubbish! She wouldn't be able to return them, and that meant that Eileen wouldn't get back her beret and the girl who owned the workbasket would lose it.

Rita went out of the room, and Monica rushed to the wastepaper basket. Where could she hide it? She could easily wait behind after sewing lesson and put it back into its place again, getting out the beret and workbasket. But where, oh, where, could she put it quickly?

The class fireplace was very big. Monica gazed at it – the chimney might be just big enough to take the wastepaper basket. Could she push it up there and hide it? Nobody would see it there?

She ran to the fireplace with the basket and tried to

shove it up the chimney. She only just managed to! How filthy her hands were now! She hoped that Rita wouldn't notice them when she came back!

Rita was so long in coming back that Monica didn't need to wait any longer. She hurried out of the room and rushed to the washroom to clean her hands. Her heart was beating fast. Goodness – what a business! First the beret – then the workbasket – then the wastepaper basket! Whatever had come over her? And *what* would Miss Brown say if she knew that the wastepaper basket was shoved high up the chimney!

She heard somebody complaining loudly in the cloakroom, which was next to the washroom. It was Eileen. 'Miss Brown told me to put on my beret and coat and go for a walk round the school garden, as I hadn't been able to play games – and I can't find my beret. Who's got it?'

Nobody had. They all looked for the beret but of course it wasn't there. *Oh, dear – it's up the chimney with the other things!* thought poor Monica. *Blow!*

How was I to know that Eileen would be sent for a walk round the garden?

Eileen grumbled and muttered, and looked everywhere. She even looked in the boot-holes – and at last pulled out a beret with a cry of triumph.

'Got it! Who put it there? Somebody jolly mean!'

Monica stared in surprise. She knew that Eileen's beret was up the chimney with the other things. Ah – perhaps it was her *own* beret that she hadn't been able to find in the morning. She ran to look. Yes – her name was sewn inside.

'That's *my* beret,' she said. 'Look, there's my name.' She hung it up on her peg. Eileen began to hunt round again, grumbling all the time. In the end there was no time for her to walk round the garden and Miss Brown was annoyed.

The bell rang for afternoon school. 'Sewing!' groaned Jack.

'Come on,' said Frances. 'I've just seen Miss Faber go by.'

Miss Faber was the sewing mistress. The children ran upstairs to the sewing room, joining up with some older ones on the way, for two classes took sewing together.

No sooner had they settled down than the trouble began. 'Miss Faber! I can't find my workbasket! It's not in the cupboard. I *know* it was there this morning!'

'Then it must be there now, Gladys,' said Miss Faber. But it wasn't, of course. It was the one that Monica had put into the wastepaper basket and shoved up the chimney!

Then someone else complained. 'My silver thimble's gone – the one my granny gave me. Miss Faber, it's gone!'

'I expect it will turn up,' said Miss Faber. 'Don't fuss so, Betty.'

Then it was Miss Faber herself who grumbled. 'Who has borrowed my scissors off my desk? I have said continually, that they must not be removed.

Whoever has my scissors must please bring them to me at once.'

Well, nobody could, of course. They were up the chimney too! Monica hung her head over her work and felt her cheeks getting redder and redder. This was dreadful.

Somebody was cutting out a little dress, and the pieces fell to the floor. 'Put them into the wastepaper basket, Harry,' said Miss Faber. 'Really, I have to tell you everything!'

Harry gathered up the snippets and went to the corner where the basket was always kept. But, of course, it wasn't there.

'It's gone,' said Harry in astonishment.

'What's gone now?' asked Miss Faber, really annoyed.

'The wastepaper basket,' said Harry, looking all round the room. 'Goodness, what a lot of things are disappearing this afternoon.'

Monica didn't dare to look up. She was so afraid

that Miss Faber would see her red face. She took out her handkerchief and pretended to blow her nose, so as to hide her red cheeks.

Something fell to the floor as she took her hanky from her pocket. It was the little silver thimble she had borrowed to use when sewing the badge on to the beret. She had popped it into her pocket and forgotten it.

The children looked to see what was rolling over the floor. 'You've dropped this out of your pocket,' said Harry, picking it up. 'Oh – why – it's Betty's silver thimble – the lovely old one her granny gave her.'

There was a dead silence in the room at once. Then Betty spoke in anger.

'My thimble! And it fell out of *your* pocket! Monica – you took it!'

'Betty! Don't talk like that,' said Miss Faber at once. 'Monica – how did you come to have that thimble? I cannot possibly believe that you meant to take it. There's surely some simple explanation?'

Monica didn't know what to say. She gazed at Miss Faber, her face scarlet and tears in her eyes. Everyone looked at her.

'I bet she knows where my workbasket is too!' said Gladys spitefully, in a low voice. Miss Faber heard her.

'That will do, Gladys,' she said '*Do* you know where Gladys's basket is, Monica?'

'And your scissors, Miss Faber!' said somebody else. 'Own up, Monica!'

Monica said nothing at all. She was absolutely tongue-tied. Miss Faber looked at her uncomfortably. *Surely* Monica hadn't taken the things – she had always seemed such a nice child. But – why didn't she answer?

The children grew impatient, and Miss Faber heard the whispering and muttering.

'Well, Monica,' she said, rising from her chair, 'I'm afraid you must come to the Headmistress with me and explain all this.'

73

'No – no!' cried Monica in horror. 'I'll tell you where everything is – it's – it's up the chimney!'

Everyone gasped in astonishment. 'Up the chimney?' said Miss Faber disbelievingly. 'But, Monica dear . . .'

'All right – I'll show you!' said Monica and burst into tears. She rushed to the chimney, put her hand up and pulled everything down. The wastepaper basket spilt its contents as it came down – and out came scissors, workbasket, beret – and all kinds of papers!

'But why did you put everything up there?' said Miss Faber, astounded.

'I'll tell you,' said poor Monica. 'I couldn't find my beret this morning so I borrowed Eileen's, though I know we're not supposed to. Its badge got torn away, so I thought I'd better mend it. I came up here to sew it on – and borrowed a workbasket, a thimble and your scissors. And then Rita came and I was scared – so I put them all into the wastepaper basket to hide them – and then I was afraid the caretaker might throw them all away into the dustbin, so I – so I shoved them up the chimney! That's all!'

Nobody said a word – it was all too surprising. Then suddenly Eileen laughed. She put her arm round Monica. 'Talk about the house-that-Jack-built! How one thing does lead to another. Don't you go shoving my beret up the chimney again!'

'Up the *chimney*!' said Jack with a little squeal. 'Oh, Monica – up the *chimney*!'

And then everyone began to laugh – even Miss Faber had to smile. But soon she rapped on her desk for silence.

'That's enough, children. The mystery is solved – but I want to tell Monica something. She hasn't behaved well, and she has a lot of people to apologise to. I'm not going to make a big thing of this, because Monica has already gone through a very bad time about it, and I think we all know she had no intention whatever of really *stealing* the things. But dear me, children – how one thing does lead to another!'

It all blew over, of course – but whenever anything is lost or missing, and somebody says, 'Wherever has it gone?', you can guess what everyone shouts in answer.

'It's up the chimney! It *must* be up the chimney!'

The Wishing Feather

The Wishing Feather

ONE DAY, when Snubby was walking along the road, he saw a pretty blue feather lying in the gutter. It had a red tip to it, and Snubby liked it.

'Just the thing to stick in my hat,' he said, and he picked up the feather and stuck it into his hat. He at once felt very grand indeed, and went whistling along the road. He didn't know that it was a wishing feather!

He passed by Dame Cooky's little shop. The dame was just setting out some hot pasties in her little window. They did look nice.

'Look at those!' said Snubby, stopping. 'I do wish I had one to eat!'

Well, of course, as he had a wishing feather in his hat, his wish came true. He suddenly felt something hot against his side, and he put his hand into his pocket in alarm to see what it was.

And in his pocket was a hot pasty! Well, well, of all the surprises! Snubby took it out and looked at it. 'I don't know where you came from, but I do know where you're going!' he said, and took an enormous bite out of the pasty.

But it was very hot and he burnt his tongue. He gave a howl that made Dame Cooky look up. She saw Snubby eating one of her pasties! Yes, there wasn't a doubt of it at all! She counted them quickly and there was one missing.

She ran out of her little shop and snatched the pasty from Snubby's hand. He was most surprised, and very cross indeed to see his lovely pasty being thrown down into the gutter and stamped on by Dame Cooky's big feet.

'You naughty little robber!' shouted Dame Cooky.

'Stealing one of my pasties and eating it under my very nose!'

'I didn't steal it!' cried Snubby. 'I wish you were in your oven, cooking with your pasties, so there!'

Well, of course, Snubby still had that wishing feather in his cap, and in a trice Dame Cooky found herself back in her kitchen – and, oh my, she was being crammed into her hot oven with the next batch of her pasties.

How she yelled and screamed! Mr Top-Hat, her next-door neighbour, ran to rescue her, and pulled her out of the oven at once.

'Do you want to cook yourself?' he said to her. 'Whatever are you trying to get into your oven for? Pooh, you smell scorched.'

'It's Snubby!' cried Dame Cooky, and she ran out into the road again. 'He wished me in my oven – and there I was! He's got hold of some magic somehow. We'd better catch him before he uses it on us all!'

Mr Top-Hat and Dame Cooky pounced on

Snubby, and shook him hard. 'Where's the magic you are using?' they cried. 'Give it up at once!'

Shake, shake, shake! Snubby's teeth rattled in his head, and his eyes nearly fell out.

'I haven't any magic!' he gasped. 'I haven't, I haven't. Let me go! Take your hands off me! I wish you hadn't got any!'

Well, in a trice Mr Top-Hat and Dame Cooky let go of Snubby – and, oh dear, they had paws instead of hands! Snubby's wish had come true. He stared at the paws, and so did they.

'My wishes are coming true,' said Snubby in a loud voice. 'I don't know why. But they are. I'm powerful! I'm important! I'm grand!'

'Wish our hands back again!' wept poor Dame Cooky. 'How am I to make pasties with paws like these? Wish our hands back again.'

'Certainly not,' said Snubby. 'It serves you both right. My word, what a time I shall have, paying people back for horrid things they've done to me!'

'Wouldn't it be better to forget all that, and pay people back for the *good* turns they have done you?' said Mr Top-Hat. 'When you have a bit of power, you want to do good, not bad, Snubby. Be careful, or you will be sorry.'

'Pooh!' said Snubby. 'You only say that because you want me to wish you back your hands. Well, I shan't. I'm going to enjoy myself now. Hallo, here comes Mr Brown. Many a time he's punished me. I'll wish him a few things to wake him up a bit!'

Mr Brown came nearer. He was the village school master, a learned and strict old fellow. Snubby let out a yell as he came up.

'Hallo, Mr Brown! I wish you had a cane running behind you to make you hurry!'

In no time at all a long, thin cane appeared behind poor Mr Brown, and hit him very smartly indeed. Mr Brown yelled and began to run. The cane hopped along too, getting in a good old smack every now and again.

Snubby jumped about for joy. 'Now I wish a whip would come and crack round his ears!' he shouted. The whip appeared, and what with its loud cracking, and the whippy little cane, poor Mr Brown had a very bad time indeed.

Then up came Dame Tick-Tock and Father Ben. Snubby greeted them with a loud shout.

'You scolded me the other day! Now I'll pay you back! You've got your best clothes on, and I wish you'd get wet through!'

Down came a shower of rain, just over poor surprised Dame Tick-Tock and Father Ben. How wet they were! It was a most surprising sight really, because no rain fell anywhere except just over the two astonished people.

Soon the word went around that Snubby had got hold of some wishing magic, and was using it. Everyone came running to see what was happening. When they saw Dame Cooky and Mr Top-Hat with paws instead of hands, and saw poor Mr Brown trying to escape from the cane and the whip, and Dame Tick-Tock and Father Ben getting wetter and wetter, they were amazed.

'Now stop this, Snubby!' cried Mr Plod the policeman. 'How dare you behave like this? I'll take you to the police station and lock you up.'

Snubby roared with laughter. 'I wish a dozen policemen would run after you and try to catch you to take *you* to the police station!' he said.

And then twelve big policemen suddenly appeared and went to put heavy hands on the astonished Mr Plod. He began to struggle with them, and got away. They ran after him. Snubby laughed till the tears ran down his cheeks.

Then people began to feel afraid. Snubby certainly had got some kind of powerful wishing magic, there was no doubt about it. And he was using it badly. There was no knowing what might happen if power was in the hands of a bad pixie who didn't know how to use it.

One by one the watching people crept away, afraid of Snubby, and scared of what he might do to them. Snubby saw them going, and he rejoiced to see how frightened everyone looked.

'Come back!' he shouted, and a great idea came into his head. 'Come back! I want to tell you something. I am very great and powerful now. I can wish for anything I want. I am the most important person in the whole of this town. I shall be your king.'

'You are not fit to be a king,' said Mr Brown, dodging the whip that cracked round his ears. 'A king should know how to use power rightly and well. You don't. And you never will.'

'I wish for *six* canes behind you!' shouted Snubby in anger. 'Aha! They will make you jump. How dare you talk to me like that?'

Everyone was silent. Snubby threw out his chest and strutted up and down. 'I am your king. I shall have a grand, golden carriage. I wish for it now, drawn by twelve black horses!'

It came, of course. One minute it wasn't there and the next it was, a fine, gleaming carriage with twelve black horses that pawed the ground impatiently. Snubby climbed into it and sat himself down, folding his arms.

'I wish for a coachman and two footmen!' he said, and, hey presto! There they were.

'And now I wish for a golden palace with a thousand windows,' shouted Snubby, feeling tremendously excited. There was a loud gasp as the watching crowd saw a beautiful palace appear on the hill nearby. Its thousand windows glittered in the sun.

Snubby gave a shout of joy. 'See that?' he yelled. 'That's my home! And I'm your king! Bow down to me, all of you! Bow down or I'll turn you into black beetles!'

Everyone except Mr Brown at once bowed themselves low to the ground. Only Mr Brown stood upright, and the cane gave him a horrid little smack. Snubby pointed his finger at Mr Brown, who had suddenly caught sight of the wishing feather in the pixie's hat. *Yes, there is no doubt about it*, thought the surprised Mr Brown, *that is a wishing feather!* How had Snubby got hold of it? And did he know he had it? The cane gave him a swipe on the legs and made him jump.

'Hey, you!' roared Snubby, still pointing his finger at Mr Brown. 'Bow down to me, do you hear? I'm your king.'

An idea flashed into Mr Brown's quick mind. 'You are not a king till you wear a cloak and a crown,' he said. 'Where is your crown?'

'That's easy!' cried Snubby. 'I wish for a cloak and fine clothes, and I wish for a golden crown!'

Away flew his old clothes and in their stead came gleaming ones of red and silver. Away flew his hat and on his head came a glittering crown. '*Now* I am your king!' cried Snubby to Mr Brown. 'Bow down!'

Mr Brown did not bow down. He watched the hat whisk away with the wishing feather in it. He knew what would happen when that was gone. All Snubby's magic would go. Ho, ho! What a shock for Snubby!

'If you don't bow down at once, I'll wish you a pair of donkey's ears!' cried Snubby in a rage, pointing his finger at Mr Brown again. 'What, you won't bow? Then I wish you had donkey's ears on you!'

But no donkey's ears came. And suddenly everything began to change. The gleaming palace on the hill faded into a mist, and all its thousand windows were gone. The lovely carriage faded too, and Snubby found himself tumbling to the ground. The horses threw up their heads, neighed and disappeared. The coachman and the footmen vanished.

Dame Cooky's hands came back, and so did Mr Top-Hat's. Dame Tick-Tock and Father Ben were no longer wet through. The twelve policemen who were after Mr Plod faded away like shadows in the sun.

And all Snubby's fine clothes disappeared, and his crown as well. But his old clothes didn't come back, nor did his hat with the lovely wishing feather. There stood poor Snubby in his holey vest and nothing else, shivering and scared. The wishing feather was gone, and his wishes would no longer come true. He could do no more magic. He had used it so badly, and this was his punishment.

'All my magic is gone!' he wailed. 'There's nothing left.'

But there *was* something left – and that was the nasty little cane that had first come to annoy Mr Brown. That hadn't gone – and now it left Mr Brown and came hopping over to Snubby. Wheee! It gave him a fine blow and made him jump in the air! Wheee!

'Don't, don't!' cried Snubby, and fled away. But the little whippy cane followed him, and everyone laughed to see Snubby leap into the air every time he was hit at.

'He could have wished a thousand good wishes,' said Mr Brown. 'Now all that is left to him is one bad one. Ah, if only I had found that wishing feather, what a wonderful lot of good I'd have done with it!'

I would too. Wouldn't you?

Who Has Won?

ONCE UPON a time the sun and the wind began to quarrel with one another.

'I am much stronger than you!' said the wind to the big round sun. 'You may be very big and very hot, but I am fierce – I can blow ships out to sea, I can blow clouds across the sky, I can . . .'

'You can do many things – but I can do more,' said the sun. 'I can do things that you can't do, although you are strong and fierce, Great Wind.'

'Tell me something you can do that I cannot!' roared the wind, making the clouds fly across the sky in fright.

'Now listen,' said the golden sun. 'Do you see that child down there? Well, do you see the coat he is wearing? Let us see who can make him take it off.'

'Easy!' shouted the wind, and the trees swayed at his great voice. 'I will try first – and I will strip off his coat in a trice! Watch me, big round sun!'

The child was walking along with his coat hanging loosely open. Suddenly the wind tore down on him and blew with all his might. WHOOOOOOOO! WHOOOOOOOO!

The child pulled his coat round him and shivered. Goodness, what a wind! He didn't like it at all.

The wind was angry to see him pull his coat tight and he swooped down again, blowing off the child's hat and almost stripping off his coat.

'Good gracious!' said the child in surprise. 'Why has the wind got up so quickly? Ooooh – how cold it is! I shall button up my coat and turn up my collar!'

So he did up every button, and then turned up his

collar. He went to pick up his hat, but the wind blew it away over a hedge.

'Horrid wind! Unkind wind!' said the child crossly. 'Stop blowing, I don't like you!'

The wind blew the other way then, and instead of having it in his face, the child had it behind him and found himself being raced along as fast as he could go.

'Stop blowing!' he cried. 'You're cold and fierce and frightening. I shall go back home and put on a thicker coat still, and button it up tightly!'

The wind was now so out of breath that he had to stop blowing.

The golden sun smiled in the sky, and called out loudly. 'Well – you couldn't get that coat off the child, could you, strong as you are, Great Wind? Now it's *my* turn! Watch how easily I can get it away from him!'

The wind was still, the clouds went slowly, so slowly over the sky, and the flags drooped on the flag poles. The sun shone steadily from the blue sky, shone on the child in his buttoned-up coat and made him feel deliciously warm.

'Ah – *that's* better!' he said. 'That horrid wind is gone. I'm warm again now. I like you, sun, shine down on me as much as you can!' He walked on happily, the sun warm on his head.

Then the sun shone even more warmly, and the child felt too hot. He unbuttoned his coat and turned down his collar.

'I'm too hot with my coat buttoned up,' he said. 'Goodness me, how hot the sun is!'

Still the sun shone steadily, making everything very warm indeed. The child began to pant with the heat, and threw his coat wide open.

'Now watch, Great Wind,' said the sun. 'Just watch!' And he sent down such hot rays that the child could hardly bear them.

'I really *must* take off my coat!' he said. 'I'm much too hot.'

And off came his coat at once. He walked along with it over his arm feeling cooler again.

'Who has won, Great Wind?' said the golden sun, pleased. 'Who has won? You with your fierceness and strength – or I with my gentle rays?'

But there was no answer. The wind had fled away to hide, and the child went home not knowing anything about the quarrel at all!

The Boy Next Door

The Boy Next Door

'DAN! DAISY! Put on your coats and go and do some shopping for me!' called Mother. 'I'm so busy today that I shan't have time to go myself.'

'Bother, bother, bother!' said Dan crossly. He was reading a most exciting book.

'I don't want to go either,' said Daisy. 'It's a horrid day, drizzling with rain. Let's wait till it stops and then go.'

Dan called to Mother. 'Oh, Mother, we don't want to go yet. It's raining.'

'That won't hurt you,' said Mother.

'I want to finish my book,' said Dan. Mother didn't

answer anything to that. She didn't call to them again, and the twins settled down to read, hoping that Mother would forget.

Now, at half past twelve they looked out into the garden and there they saw something that surprised them very much! It was fine now, and a boy was pedalling up the path to the door, with a basket on the front of his tricycle.

'Why! That's our tricycle! It must have come back from being mended!' said Dan. 'Hurrah. Now we can play with it. But what's the boy next door doing, riding it? What cheek!'

They ran downstairs to see. Mother was at the front door, taking a basket of goods from John, the boy from next door.

'What are you doing with our tricycle?' said Dan.

'John kindly offered to do my shopping for me,' said Mother. 'He was doing some for his own mother, and he said he'd do mine too. Your tricycle was brought back just when John was talking to me, so I said he could ride it down to the village and do the shopping more quickly.'

'It's a marvellous tricycle!' said John, beaming. 'Your mother says I can have it this afternoon too, because I'm doing my granny's shopping then.'

'Oh,' said Dan and Daisy. They went very red indeed. John tricycled down the path, and Mother shut the front door.

'We're not very nice children, are we?' said Dan. 'I'm sorry, Mother. Don't think John's nicer than us! We'll do *all* your shopping tomorrow!'

Bicycle Magic

Bicycle Magic

'IF I could only get hold of Slippery-One, I'd soon pop him into prison,' said Mr Grim the policeman.

'That's just it,' said Wriggles the pixie. 'He always seems to get away with things! He's too clever. If he steals anything he pretends it was given to him – or he took it by mistake – or he's so clever that nobody *knows* he's stolen it, though we all think he has!'

'We want a bit of magic to deal with him!' said Derry the goblin. 'If you're dealing with clever people, you've got to be clever yourself.'

'Well,' said Wriggles to Derry, '*we're* clever, aren't we? We ought to be able to get the better of

Slippery-One. We'd better try!' So they went off together and thought very hard. And then Wriggles had an idea.

'Suppose Slippery-One came along and saw me with a very fine bicycle, what do you think he would do?' he said to Derry.

'Borrow it,' said Derry at once. 'Borrow it and never give it back! But you haven't *got* a fine new bicycle, Wriggles.'

'No. But I could have if you'd let me do a little magic,' said Wriggles.

'What do you mean?' asked Derry.

'Well,' said Wriggles, 'I know how to turn people into bicycles, Derry – but only if they'll *let* me. I suppose you wouldn't let me turn *you* into one, would you? Just for an hour or two, until we've caught Slippery-One properly. I promise to turn you back into yourself after that.'

Derry looked rather doubtful. 'Are you sure you *could* turn me back into myself?' he asked. 'I don't want to live in the shed for the rest of my life and be ridden by you all day long.'

'Oh, Derry, as if I'd do such a thing as that!' said Wriggles. 'You know I wouldn't. I'm your best friend, aren't I?'

'Yes, you are,' said Derry. 'Well, I'll trust you then. But what's your idea?'

'Listen,' said Wriggles, getting excited. 'I'll turn you into a shining new bicycle and I'll ride you down the road where Slippery-One lives – then I'll get off and lean you against the fence by his house and do up my shoelace or something . . .'

'And Slippery-One is sure to come out and borrow the bicycle – borrow *me*, because I'll be the bicycle!' said Derry. 'And I'll go straight off to the police station with him! We'll warn Mr Grim to expect us. Oh my, what fun!'

Well, the next thing was for Wriggles to change Derry into a new bicycle. He knew the spell, and, if Derry was willing, it would work all right. And, sure enough, it did! Derry suddenly changed into a very fine new bicycle, with a gleaming pair of wheels, a shining bell and a pair of rubber pedals that could make the bicycle go very fast indeed.

'Oh, Derry, you look beautiful!' said Wriggles, and he got on to the saddle. The bell rang. That was the only way Derry had of talking now! Whenever he wanted to get Wriggle's attention Derry rang his own bell! R-r-r-r-r-ring!

Wriggles rode off. He came into the road where Slippery-One lived, and then, just by the pixie's house, he got off the bicycle and leant it against the fence.

He bent down as if he was doing up his shoe. Slippery-One spotted the shining new bicycle at once and his eyes gleamed. He came out of his front door.

'Hallo, Wriggles,' he said. 'That's a wonderful new bike you've got.'

'Isn't it!' said Wriggles. 'Have a look at it. Brand new today!'

Slippery-One longed to have a bicycle just like

that. 'Can I ring the bell?' he said, and he rang it. 'Oh, what a lovely bell!'

Then he touched the lamp. 'Will it light?' he asked. 'Can I put it on? Oh, what a fine light it gives!'

Then he saw the pump. 'I say, what a fine black pump! Do let me just pump up one of the tyres to see how well the pump works.'

'Certainly, certainly!' said Wriggles, so Slippery-One pumped up the back tyre.

Then he ran his hand over the saddle. 'What a nice saddle! Could I just sit on it for a moment?'

'Of course!' said Wriggles, so Slippery-One sat on the saddle, balancing himself by holding with one hand to the fence. He worked the pedals round and round with his feet.

'What nice pedals!' he said. 'I say, Wriggles, let me just ride to the end of the road and back for a treat, will you?'

'Yes, yes, certainly,' said Wriggles and winked to himself. Wasn't that just what he knew Slippery-One would say? And didn't he know that the pixie was planning to ride off with the bicycle, hide it somewhere, and then come back with a long story about someone stealing it from him? Ho, ho – he knew Slippery-One all right! The pixie set off on the bicycle. He rode to the corner – but he didn't turn round and come back. No, he went straight on! He knew a place on the common where he could hide the bicycle. But the bicycle wouldn't go there. To Slippery-One's great surprise it began to ring its bell violently and to go very fast indeed! It turned a corner Slippery-One didn't want to turn. It went a way he didn't want it to go. It was a most extraordinary and most annoying bicycle.

Slippery-One felt frightened. But he couldn't get off because the bicycle was going much too fast, and it took no notice of the brakes at all! Slippery-One felt very scared indeed.

'Where are you going?' he yelled to the bicycle. And the bell rang in answer, 'R-r-r-ring!' But

Slippery-One didn't know what it meant.

The bicycle rode straight to the police station and, oh my goodness, it rode straight up the steps, bump-bump-bump, and into the big room where Mr Grim and two other policemen were waiting! It stopped suddenly and Slippery-One fell off.

'Thank you, Derry,' said Mr Grim and clapped his hand on Slippery-One's shoulder. The pixie stared round in surprise. Derry? Where was Derry? 'R-r-r-r-ring!' said the bicycle bell, and then suddenly Wriggles ran into the police station and gave the brown saddle a hearty smack.

'*Bilderoonapookyliptikinna!*' he cried, which is the magic word used for turning bicycles back into people.

'*Bilderoonapookyliptikinna!*'

And at once Derry changed from the bicycle back to himself again. You should have seen Slippery-One's astonished face.

'So that was why you wouldn't go the way I wanted you to!' he said at last. Derry grinned.

'That was why!' he said. 'My word, you're heavy, Slippery-One. I shouldn't like to carry you for long!'

'Say goodbye to him,' boomed Mr Grim. 'You won't be seeing him for quite a while. Come along with me, Slippery-One. Your slippery days are over.'

And that was the last the village saw of him for a very long time. As for Derry, he was made quite a hero, but when people begged him to turn into a bicycle and let them ride him, he shook his head.

'No, thank you!' he said. 'I might get a puncture – and then when I turned back into myself again I'd have a hole in one of my feet! No, thank you!'

The Kind Little Girl

The Kind Little Girl

A GOOD many birds lived in Mary's garden. They liked Mary. She never pulled their nests to pieces, or took their eggs. She liked listening to their songs, and she knew all their names.

The robin lived in her garden, and the stumpy little wren. The blackbird lived there, and the thrush. Many starlings came down to bathe in Mary's pond and sat in the trees afterwards to chatter and dry their wings.

Now it was wintertime. The days were cold and the nights were colder still. Then one day the snow came and the birds saw that the ground was white instead of green and brown.

There was very little food to be found. The berries had been pulled from the bushes and trees, and now there were very few. It was cold, so cold!

'I can hardly uncurl my toes from the twig when I wake up in the morning!' said one sparrow to another.

'And did you know that all the puddles are frozen hard and the pond is made of ice too?' said a listening blackbird. 'There is nothing to drink. I am so thirsty.'

'We are hungry and thirsty and cold!' said the robin. 'We shall die. This is a terrible time for us. What shall we do?'

'There is only one thing to do,' said the freckled thrush. 'We must tell that kind little girl our troubles. Surely she will help us!'

So what do you think they all did? They went and sat in a row on the fence, fluffing out their feathers to keep themselves warm and looking as miserable as could be!

Mary saw them. 'Poor little creatures!' she cried.

'Are you so cold and hungry? I will look after you till this bitter weather has gone!'

She made a bird table for them – just a sheet of board nailed to a little pole. On the table she put all the scraps her mother could spare – crumbs, scrapings from the milk puddings, a bone or two, and some berries she had picked and dried to give the birds in winter. She put a big enamel basin of water on the bird table, so that they might drink. Each bird took a delicious sip and held his head back to let the water trickle down his throat. They pecked at the food hungrily and wanted to sing a thank-you song to Mary, but they couldn't see her.

'She's making warm beds for us!' sang the thrush. 'Look – she's got flowerpots to hide in the hedge, and she's stuffed them with straw or moss. Isn't she kind?'

She was kind, wasn't she, and it's no wonder they all sing songs to her in springtime. Would you like to do all that Mary did? You can if you like!

Harry's Fine Idea

Harry's Fine Idea

DADDY WAS opening his letters at the breakfast table. 'I do hope there's one from Captain Halling,' he said. 'I've got to go and see him about a book he's writing on ships, and he said he'd send me a carefully drawn map to show me how to get to his place.'

'It's right in the country, isn't it?' said Mummy. 'It should be fun to go there. He has such a wonderful collection of model ships that he's made, hasn't he?'

'Oh, Daddy, is that the Captain Halling you were telling me about, who's made models of all the famous ships there are?' asked Harry, pricking up his ears. 'Oh, Daddy, do, *do* take me with you. You know how I love ships. I would *so* like to see his models. I wouldn't be a nuisance, I promise you.'

'No. You can't come,' said Daddy, opening his last letter. 'I may get back late.'

'Oh, let him come,' said Mummy. 'It wouldn't matter his being late just for once. He does so love ships, and I'm sure Captain Halling wouldn't mind Harry seeing them all.'

'I said *no*,' said Daddy. 'He hasn't been working hard at school lately, and doesn't deserve a treat. Now if he'd been top of his form this week, I *might* have let him go with me, as today is a Saturday.'

'Oh, Daddy, I *promise* you I'll be top next week!' said Harry at once.

'I've heard promises like that before,' said Daddy. 'No – I've been a bit disappointed in you lately, Harry. You can't come.'

Harry looked sulky and kicked the table leg, which made Mummy frown at him. Daddy hated sulks. But he was busy looking at his last letter and studying a map that had come with it.

'Ah, here's the map from Captain Halling,' he said, pleased. 'Beautifully drawn too – as neatly done as the plans he draws of those lovely model ships of his! Well, I ought to be able to get to his place without losing my way now!'

Daddy picked up the newspaper and began to read it. Then he finished his toast and drank his coffee. He picked up all his letters, put some into his pocket and carefully tore up two into little pieces and threw them into the wastepaper basket. Then he went out to get his car ready for the journey to see Captain Halling.

He came back in a few minutes looking very worried. 'I believe I must have put the two letters into the wastepaper basket that I wanted to keep,' he said, 'and kept the others that didn't need answering. I do hope I haven't torn up the one with the map in it.'

'I'll look, Daddy,' said Harry, and took the little torn-up pieces out of the basket. He sorted them out on the table.

'Oh, Daddy – yes, you have!' he said. 'I can see tiny bits of the map here, all mixed up with the pieces of the other letter. What a pity you tore them up so very, very small!'

'That *is* a *nuisance*!' said Daddy. 'Well, I'll just have to make my way as best I can, and hope that I shan't get lost. How careless of me!'

'I'm going to make you some sandwiches to take with you, dear,' said Mummy. 'How soon will you be ready?'

'In about three-quarters of an hour,' said Daddy, going out again.

Harry gathered up the torn letters and took them back to the basket. Then he stopped and looked at them. *I wonder if I could possibly put the map together for Daddy – and stick all the bits on to a sheet of paper, to make the map again?* he thought. *After all, it's really only like a jigsaw puzzle – many little bits that make a whole – and I'm good at doing those!*

He went back to the table, which Mummy had

cleared now, and sat down. It didn't take him long to sort out one letter from another. For one thing the envelope and sheet of one letter were a cream colour, but Captain Halling's sheets and envelope were white.

Next, he sorted out the bits of white envelope and put them on one side. Then he found the bits that belonged to the letter itself – and that left only the pieces of the torn-up map. 'About thirty,' said Harry to himself. 'Well, I've done jigsaws of two hundred pieces, so this oughtn't to take me long! Poor Daddy – he'd be sure to get lost without this map, because Captain Halling lives in such an out-of-the-way place.'

He set to work – but it wasn't nearly as easy as doing a proper jigsaw puzzle, whose pieces were of thick cardboard, or of wood, easy to fit into one another. The bits of paper didn't fit in – they only touched or joined, and moved so easily that Harry kept having to start again.

At last he had half done – and then a terrible thing happened. Quite suddenly he sneezed! And to his dismay, all the bits he had matched together flew off the table at once!

Now I've got to begin all over again! he thought, and felt quite in despair. Then he had a good idea. He would get a big sheet of paper and a pot of paste, and each time he found a bit that he could join on to another piece, he would *paste* it on to the paper – then if he sneezed or coughed, the pieces would stay put and not blow away!

This really was a splendid idea, and Harry got on well. He had almost finished when Mummy came in. 'What in the world are you doing?' she said. 'Oh, *Harry* – why, that's the map Daddy tore into little pieces, isn't it? And you've put them together again and pasted them on a sheet of paper. Why, Daddy can easily use it now!'

'I've just got these last two bits to paste on,' said Harry. 'I hope Daddy isn't leaving yet! Tell him not to go without seeing me, Mummy – but don't tell him why!'

So Mummy called out to Daddy. 'Come in and say

goodbye to us before you go, dear!'

Daddy came in after about three minutes, all ready to go. He kissed Mummy. 'Expect me back when you see me!' he said. 'I'm sure to get lost without the map. Goodbye, Harry.'

'Daddy, look – I've put the map together again for you!' said Harry, his face red with excitement. 'You won't lose your way now! I got every piece out of the wastepaper basket.'

Daddy picked up the map, with all the bits and pieces so neatly pasted on to the big sheet of writing paper. He stared at it in wonder. Then he looked at Harry.

'Do you mean to say you've been at work on this ever since breakfast?' he said. 'Even though I scolded you for not doing well at school?'

'Yes, but I knew you might get lost without the map, and you'd be worried,' said Harry. 'And I'm good at jigsaws, so I suddenly got the idea of doing this.'

'But it's marvellous!' said Daddy. 'Even the tiniest

bit beautifully pasted on and joined to the next! And you did it all so quickly!'

'I could have been quicker, but I suddenly sneezed and all the bits flew on to the floor!' said Harry, and that made Daddy roar with laughter. He clapped Harry on the back.

'What about that promise of yours to be top of the form next week?' he said. 'Did you really mean it?'

'Yes, of course I did,' said Harry.

'All right, I'll believe you this time,' said Daddy. 'I'll take you at your word. Buck up, and get your cap and overcoat. I'll take you with me after all! You deserve it after having such a good idea!'

'Oh, DADDY!' cried Harry in delight, and sped off to get his out-of-door things. What a wonderful surprise! How lucky that he hadn't felt too cross to piece together the map for Daddy. If he had sulked, he wouldn't have done it, and how silly that would have been!

Mummy was very pleased too. She brushed his overcoat for him, and gave him some extra sandwiches and an apple. 'And mind you read that map properly for Daddy, and be sure he takes the right road!' she said. 'Well, goodbye – and enjoy yourselves!'

Off they went, Harry sitting proudly beside his father, the map ready to use in front of him as soon as it should be needed. It was fun to go out with Daddy. He was a first-class driver, and drove fast, which Harry liked.

A whole day with his father! And to think he was going to see the wonderful model ships that Captain Halling had made!

'Now you can tell me the way by your map,' said Daddy at last. And Harry at once took it up and guided his father proudly. 'Turn to the left here. Now straight on. Turn right after the next railway bridge. Straight on now for about two miles, then look for a big church ... sharp right now, Daddy, then straight on for about five miles ...'

Harry had a wonderful day. Captain Halling was delighted to see him, and Harry and his father looked at the lovely models to their hearts' content. Ships of all kinds, old-fashioned and new. Models of steamers. Models of the two newest liners. Battleships, cruisers – Harry had never had such an interesting day in his life!

'Well, I'm glad your father thought of bringing you with him,' said old Captain Halling. 'Here's a little model to take back – it's one of the old schooners, properly rigged.'

Harry couldn't believe it. Whatever would the boys at school say when he showed them this? He thanked Captain Halling over and over again.

Then back home he went with his father, happy and tired. Oh, what a good thing he had pasted up that map for Daddy that morning! As for being top of the form next week, well he'd be top for the *rest of the term*, not just one week! That would show Daddy he could keep his word!

He will too, I'm quite sure of that!

The Little Girl Who Was Shy

The Little Girl Who Was Shy

THERE WAS once a little girl called Janet who was very shy. She was so shy that she couldn't even shake hands, or say 'Quite well, thank you,' when people spoke to her. And even if people asked her how her dolls were, or if she liked sweets, she still didn't say a word.

Janet wished and wished she wasn't shy, but she just *couldn't* seem to make her tongue talk when visitors came.

Now one day Janet went out with her auntie. They went into the fields, and Auntie sat down with her back against a tree to do some sewing.

'You run about and play,' she said to Janet. Janet ran off a little way and then came back to show Auntie something she had found.

But her aunt was fast asleep! Janet didn't like to wake her up. She ran off again – and suddenly, just behind a big blackberry bush, she saw about twelve very small people. They were all walking along, talking in tiny high voices, rather like the swallows do.

Janet stared in great surprise. She thought they must be fairy folk, they were so small. They looked up at her and smiled.

'Good afternoon,' said a little fairy girl. 'What's your name?'

Well, of course, Janet was too shy to say her name! She just went red and said nothing.

'We are going to Jinky's birthday party,' said another fairy. 'Would you like to see what I'm taking him for a present?'

Janet was simply longing to see the present, but her tongue wouldn't say a word.

'Would you like to come with us, little girl?' said a third little person. 'Jinky would like to see you.'

Well, Janet would have liked that better than anything else in the world – but she still didn't answer. Then the fairies began to talk to one another in surprise.

'She doesn't speak! She doesn't say a word!'

'Do you suppose she has a tongue?'

'Poor little girl! She can't talk. And she looks such a dear little girl too. What can we do about it?'

'Have you a tongue, little girl?' asked the first fairy. Still Janet didn't answer. She really was a little silly, wasn't she?

The fairies talked again. 'We can't give her a tongue, because she's so tall and big. We'd never reach up to her mouth.'

'Well, look at her shoes,' said another fairy. 'They are nice little lace shoes – and they each have tongues! We could make those talk instead of Janet. Then, when people ask her questions, the tongues of her shoes can answer for her. That would be a help to her.'

Before Janet could take away her feet, one of the fairies had rubbed something on to the tongue of each shoe. Then they spoke to Janet.

'Can you speak now, little girl?'

And to Janet's enormous surprise, a voice answered from down near her feet – a funny deep voice. 'Yes, thank you. I can speak!'

It gave the little girl such a shock that she ran away at once. She ran to her aunt, who opened her eyes.

'Is anything wrong?' she asked Janet. Janet didn't like to tell Auntie about the tongues in her shoes being able to talk, so she said nothing. But the tongues answered at once.

'No, nothing is the matter, thank you, Auntie.'

Her aunt was surprised to hear such a deep voice. 'Why, it sounds as if your voice has gone down to your shoes!' she said. 'Come along now – it's time to go home.'

They went home – and Mummy had visitors! Janet was taken in to see them.

'Oh! So this is Janet!' said Mrs Brown. 'How do you do, Janet?'

Well, Janet felt shy, of course, and couldn't say a word. But that didn't matter! Her shoes answered cheerfully for her.

'I'm quite well, thank you!'

'What a well-mannered child – but what a deep voice!' said Mrs Jones. 'And how are all your dolls, my dear?'

Janet didn't answer, but hung down her head. The tongues of her shoes spoke up well, quite enjoying themselves.

'Oh, my doll Angela has a bad cold, and is in bed. Josephine has the measles, and Hilary has fallen down and hurt her knee so that I had to bandage it.'

Now all this wasn't a bit true, and Janet felt really ashamed of her shoes for telling such stories. All the visitors laughed.

'Janet's voice seems to come up from her boots!' said Mrs Harris. 'Well, my dear, what are you going to have for your tea?'

The shoes answered happily. 'Sardine sandwiches, chocolate buns, ginger biscuits and ginger beer!'

'Oh, Janet! Don't tell such naughty stories!' said Mummy, quite shocked. 'You had better go back to the nursery. I do like you to speak when you are spoken to, but not to tell stories like that.'

Janet ran out of the room, angry with her shoes. On the way to the nursery she met Cook's sister, who had come to tea. Cook's sister liked children and she spoke to Janet kindly.

'And where have you been for your walk today, my dear?'

Janet was too shy to say a word – but the shoes spoke up at once. 'Oh, I went to the farm and over the hill and down by the shops, and home by the fields – quite six miles!'

'Dear me!' said Cook's sister, surprised. 'That

seems too long a walk for a little girl like you!'

'Janet! What stories!' said Auntie, who was in the playroom nearby. 'Why, we only went to the fields! Come along now and wash your hands for tea.'

Janet really felt very, very cross with her shoes. *Next time anybody asks me anything, I'll answer before my shoes do, so that they can't get in their naughty stories first!* she thought. So, when a friend of Mummy's came in after tea and spoke to her, Janet answered at once.

'And what did you have for your tea?' asked Mummy's friend.

'Brown bread-and-butter and two biscuits,' said Janet at once, before the shoes could speak.

'There's a good girl, to answer so nicely,' said Auntie, pleased. 'You can have a sweet for that.'

Janet was delighted. She looked down at her shoes. The tongues wagged themselves a little, as if they were cross.

'Does Janet know her alphabet?' asked Mummy's friend. 'Could she say it to me?'

'She knows it very well – but she will never say it for anybody, she's so shy,' said Auntie.

Janet thought she had better say it at once, before her shoe tongues said it all wrong. So she opened her mouth and said her alphabet beautifully. Auntie listened in the greatest surprise. Mummy's friend clapped her hands when Janet had finished.

'Clever girl! Here are two shillings for you! I never thought you could say a thing so nicely. I always thought you were rather a silly little girl before, who couldn't say boo to a goose!'

Two shillings! Janet was very pleased. She began to think that it was a very good idea to speak when she was spoken to, and to be polite and well-mannered. It was nice to be thought a clever, good little girl. And she just *wouldn't* let those shoes of hers say another word!

Well, you know, she didn't! As soon as anyone spoke to her all that week, Janet had an answer ready, and soon people didn't say any more that she was shy.

They just said what a well-mannered, nicely spoken child she was, and they gave her sweets and smiled at her kindly. Janet enjoyed it all very much.

How silly I was to be shy! she thought. *It is much easier not to be. I never will be again – and those shoe tongues will never, never get another chance to say a word!*

They didn't – and they were really very cross about it. When the shoes had to be mended next time, Mummy said she thought Janet had better have a new pair, because her feet had grown.

'We'll give these away,' she said. 'They are very good shoes still.' So the shoes were given away, and I do wonder if they went to a shy child. What a shock she will get, won't she, when the tongues begin to talk!

The Biggest Piece
of Luck

The Biggest Piece
of Luck

'I DO wish you had more friends, Ronnie,' said his mother, looking up from her sewing. 'There you sit in your corner, poring over some nature book or other. Why don't you go and play with the other children?'

'I'm all right, Mother,' said Ronnie, wishing that his mother wouldn't so often talk about playing with others. 'I like being by myself.'

'Well, I *don't* like it,' said his mother. 'Don't the others like you? Or don't you like them? You ought to be going out to tea and bringing friends here.'

Ronnie didn't answer. He just went on reading, hoping that his mother wouldn't bother him any more. But she went on again.

'Mrs Brown was telling me what fun her two children have with three others – they've got a club of some sort and have regular meetings down in the shed at the bottom of their garden. They have a password and . . .'

'Yes, I know, Mother!' said Ronnie. 'And John Harris has a club too, with passwords and a meeting place – and there's a secret society at school as well – but nobody asks me to join them, and *I'm* not going to push myself where I'm not wanted!'

'Not wanted! But why shouldn't they want you?' said his mother, astonished. 'You're not selfish or mean or rough, or . . .'

'It's just because I'm quiet, and I like things they don't,' said Ronnie desperately. 'I like watching birds, and you have to be quiet for that. I like going down to the pond and watching the water voles plop in and out and the moorhens bob down under the water and come up again. The others only like noisy, shouting games, and I don't like too much of that. *Please* don't say any more.'

'Well, I'm going to,' said his mother. 'I don't like seeing a decent boy like you left out of everything. Do you know what *I* think, Ronnie? I think *you* need to be noisy and play exciting games, *you* need to be one of a club and help in it – and the others need to be quiet sometimes, and learn to watch things as you do, and love them. I should have thought that any little club would be glad of you.'

'Oh, Mother – you don't understand,' said poor Ronnie. 'You may be right, but how *can* I push myself in when I'm not really wanted? I tell you they don't *want* quiet boys like me, they want – well, they want adventurous sort of people – you know, brave and plucky and daring and all that – and I'm not.'

'Well, I shan't say any more,' said his mother impatiently. 'But I do long to have you ask a little crowd of friends here, so that I can give them a fine tea and hear you playing in the garden afterwards!

You're an only child and I want you to have friends.'

After that Ronnie's mother said no more and Ronnie heaved a sigh of relief. He *wanted* to be in a club, really, he badly longed for real friends, he wanted someone to share his love of birds and animals – but he simply *couldn't* push himself anywhere that he wasn't wanted. It was no good – he couldn't.

The next afternoon was a half-holiday. Ronnie listened to the others arranging what they were going to do.

'Meet in our shed, half past two sharp, club members!' said George. 'And, Harry, if you forget the password again, you won't be admitted!'

'Secret Six Society – meet at our treehouse at quarter to three,' he heard Jane say. 'Bring biscuits if you can and something to drink. Wear your badges, of course.'

It really seemed as if everyone was arranging something to do except Ronnie! He went off alone as he usually did, and began to plan what *he* would do.

I'll go and watch the swans and the moorhens on the lake, he thought. *And I might take a jar with me and see if I can bring something interesting home for my aquarium. I'll watch the swallows skimming the water for flies too – they'll soon be flying away to warmer countries and it may be the last time I can watch them.*

'Going off alone as usual?' said his mother after Ronnie had had his lunch. 'It's a shame, Ronnie!'

'Oh, I like it,' said Ronnie, and off he went with a little jar on a string. The lake was a good way away, and he enjoyed the walk. He got there at last and sat down quietly under a tree. Now, where were those moorhens?

'None to be seen – they will be swimming under the water I expect,' said Ronnie. 'Their heads will pop up in a minute, and then their bodies!'

He was right. Suddenly four or five little black heads popped up above the surface of the water, and then a whole family of moorhens appeared, calling 'crek-crek' to one another, and swimming off fast, their heads bobbing like clockwork.

I wish I had someone to watch with me, thought Ronnie. *Oh, there's a water vole. Plop! He's dived into the water!*

It was while he was sitting quite still, and not making even a small movement, that Ronnie heard a noise some way off. At first he took no notice. Then, as it came again and again, he sat up straight and listened. What could it be?

It sounded like a faint shouting. It went on and on, then stopped. Then it began again. Ronnie felt uneasy.

It can't be someone in trouble, surely? he thought. *Ah, it's stopped again. Perhaps it was just children playing somewhere.*

But soon the far-off shouting began again, and Ronnie stood up. Blow! What was it? He didn't want to leave this peaceful, interesting corner by the lake, but he knew quite well that if someone wanted help, he must go and find out what he could do about it! He stood and listened and then went off in the direction of the sound.

Soon, he saw a house hidden in some trees. It was the only house for some distance, and it seemed as if the shouts were coming from there. He read the name on the gate – RED CHIMNEYS.

Why, surely that's where George lives! he thought. *Yes, it is. My word, what yells! Whatever's the matter?*

He soon found out! He went right round the house and came to the back. From a window high up near the roof he heard the yells, and then someone leant out of the window. It was George!

'Hey! Good gracious, it is really *you*, Ronnie! What a bit of luck!'

'What's the matter?' shouted back Ronnie, astonished. 'Why are you shouting?'

Three more heads poked out of the window beside George's. Ronnie saw Tom, Katie and Pat, all members of the Four-Leaved Clover Club. George shouted again.

'Ronnie! Our club met this afternoon, but we couldn't meet in the shed as usual – so we thought we'd meet up here in the attic – but the door's got jammed and we can't get out. Can you come up and help?'

'But where's your mother?' asked Ronnie.

'She's out. There's nobody here but us this afternoon. Ronnie, come in at the back door, for goodness' sake, and help us. We've been here ages.'

Ronnie waved his hand and ran to the back door. He opened it, went inside and found his way to the stairs. Up he went to the first floor, and then up again to the attic. There were two rooms there, one with its door open, the other with its door shut. Behind the door he could hear the voices of the Four-Leaved Clover Club members. He banged on the door.

'I'm here. Shall I shove at the door?'

'Yes. Shove hard, and we'll pull!' said George from inside. So Ronnie shoved and George pulled – but all that happened was that the handle of the door came off in George's hand, and he fell over with a terrific bump!

'Hey – wait a minute – there's a key here,' called Ronnie. 'Maybe when you went in and banged the door it half-locked like keys do sometimes. Wait – I'll see. Yes, I believe it has. There, I've turned it!'

The door came open at once, and all the club members rushed out, glad to be free. George gave Ronnie a clap on the back.

'Thanks! A hundred thousand thanks! My mother doesn't come back till six, and our cook, who's gone out for a couple of hours, is deaf, and she wouldn't have heard our shouts even when she got back. We'd have been prisoners for hours! Come on, let's go downstairs.'

'Good old Ronnie!' said Tom. 'Whatever are you doing in this direction? How did you manage to hear our shouts?'

Ronnie told him. 'I just came to watch the swans and moorhens on the lake, and to get something for my aquarium,' he said. 'And I heard shouts.'

'I say, Ronnie – you know an awful lot about nature, don't you?' said Katie. 'Our club used to go for nature walks and keep a bird table and things like that, when Fanny was a member. But she's gone away now and the club's not nearly so interesting.'

'It's no good asking *you* to join us, is it, Ronnie?' said George suddenly. 'Do you know enough nature to teach us about birds, and to help us to make an aquarium? I've got a fine glass tank, but we simply don't know how to arrange it for an aquarium.'

'Ronnie doesn't belong to *any* clubs – do you, Ronnie?' said Pat. 'You just keep yourself to yourself, don't you? I bet clubs bore you!'

'Well,' said Ronnie and stopped. 'You see, I ...'

'Look – we badly need a member who knows about nature,' said George, taking Ronnie's arm. 'Can't you do us a favour and belong to a club, just for once? It's fun to share things, Ronnie – and have a secret password and a badge and a meeting place and nice little feasts – and make things and learn things. Honestly it is. *Do* belong.'

'Well,' began Ronnie again, quite overcome by all this. 'Well, I'd *love* to. Nobody ever asked me before. I thought I was too quiet to belong to a club, I thought nobody wanted me. Gosh, yes – I'd love to show you how to make an aquarium – and you could come with me and collect things from the pond for it ...'

'And can you make a wormery?' asked Pat. 'I want one of those. And ...'

'We'll make you a member straight away!' said George, seeing how pleased Ronnie looked. 'My word, this is a scoop for us – getting old Ronnie for our club! I know the Secret Six thought of asking you when Kenneth left them, but they thought you turned up your nose at clubs, so they asked Doris instead. And now *we've* got you!'

Ronnie was red with excitement. Why, he hadn't guessed that anyone had even *thought* of wanting him!

What *would* his mother say? He would ask the whole club to his home for tea on Saturday! He would join in their fun and games – and they would share his interest in birds and animals and all the rest. His mother was right after all!

'Let's go back to the attic!' said Tom. 'We'll make Ronnie a member *at once* before he changes his mind. You have to promise two or three things very solemnly, Ronnie. I hope you won't mind.'

Ronnie was ready to promise anything! He looked at the little four-leaved clover badges that the others wore – buttons covered with white material on which a four-leaved clover was worked in green. He was sure his mother could make him one that very night! How many many times had he envied George and the others when he had seen that badge on their chests!

They all went back to the attic. They took the key from the outside of the door and put it into the keyhole on the inside, so that the lock couldn't slip again. Then they shut the door and sat down in a ring.

I must not tell you what happened then because it is always a special and secret meeting when the Four-Leaved Clover Club elect a new member and he makes his promises and learns the password.

But I *can* tell you that Ronnie is a great success in the club, and that his mother has made him a very fine badge indeed, most beautifully embroidered with a four-leaved clover. And once a fortnight Ronnie asks all the other members to tea, and they meet in an old cellar under his house and make a most terrific noise.

Then his mother smiles a secret smile. Yes, she was right after all, as mothers so often are! Ronnie had learnt to laugh and shout and share with the others – and they too were sharing in all the things that Ronnie knew and loved. That lovely aquarium made out of George's old tank – the wormery he had shown Pat how to make – and the injured hedgehog Katie had found and that Ronnie had tamed and made into the club's mascot – what fun they had all had with one another!

'We called our club the Four-Leaved Clover Club because we thought it might be a lucky club, with that name,' said George to Ronnie. 'But our biggest piece of luck was when my attic door got stuck, and you came along to rescue us, Ronnie – and made you belong to the club!'

'It was *my* biggest piece of luck too,' said Ronnie. And he was right – it was!

Annie Gets Into
Trouble

Annie Gets Into Trouble

'WHERE ARE you going, Annie?' called Mark, as he saw Annie running down the road.

'To the shops,' said Annie. 'My granny's ill and I'm going to buy her some violets. I've got sixpence, look – I took it out of my moneybox.'

'Sixpence! That won't buy many violets!' said Mark scornfully. 'Spend it on sweets – you'll get more sweets than you will violets!'

'No. My granny likes flowers,' said Annie. 'She loves daffodils best of all in the springtime, but they are so dear.'

'Daffodils? Oh, I can show you plenty of those,'

said Mark at once.

'I expect you can – in somebody's garden!' said Annie. 'Don't be silly!'

'No. In a wood, I mean,' said Mark. 'Honestly, Annie! They're growing under the trees, as wild as you like. I saw them yesterday.'

'Well, why didn't you pick them then?' said Annie.

'Because I don't waste *my* time picking flowers,' said Mark. 'What do I want with daffodils? Listen, Annie – if I show you where these wild daffodils grow, so that you can pick a bunch for your granny, will you buy some sweets with that sixpence and share them with me?'

'All right,' said Annie. 'But I'll be very cross with you if you take my sweets and *don't* show me those wild daffodils! I shall tell my mother if you cheat me.'

'Oh, come on,' said Mark. 'Let's go and buy the sweets first. The sweet shop is on the way to this daffodil place.'

So they went first to the sweet shop, and Annie

bought a bag of toffees. The two divided them outside the shop, and Mark put half in his pockets.

'Now show me the daffodils,' said Annie. Mark set off down the road, round the corner, up a hill and down again. They passed some very big houses, and then Mark led Annie along beside a low fence.

'There you are!' he said, pointing to where clumps of yellow daffodils grew under the shade of big trees. 'See? All growing wild in the grass!'

'But they can't be wild,' said Annie. 'Why is this fence round the wood? It must be to keep people out.'

'There's a gate in the fence round the corner,' said Mark. 'If it's open, it means that anyone can go into the wood and pick. You wait here. I'll go and see if it's open. If it is, I'll give you a shout.'

He ran off round the corner. He came to a little gate – fast shut! He undid it and swung it open. Then he shouted loudly.

'Come on, Annie! It's all right, the gate's open!' Annie ran round the corner and came to where the little gate was swinging to and fro.

'See? What did I tell you?' said Mark. 'Now you go and pick a nice big bunch.'

'It seems funny to be able to pick as many daffodils as I like even when they're growing wild in the grass like that,' said Annie. 'You come and pick some for your mother too, Mark.'

'No thanks. It's a waste of time picking flowers. I told you that before,' said Mark. 'Well, I'll leave you to it. Goodbye!'

He ran off at top speed, putting a toffee into his mouth and grinning to himself. Silly Annie! Anyone could take her in! Fancy believing him when he said that if the gate was open, anyone could go in and pick the daffodils! Well, she would have her daffodils – and he had got his toffees – so that was fine!

Annie was having a fine time picking the lovely golden daffodils. She picked carefully, choosing many that were only half-out, knowing that Granny liked to watch them come out slowly and beautifully.

'There! I've got about twenty!' she said at last. 'That's enough. I mustn't be greedy. I must leave plenty for other people.'

She was just picking a few of the long thin leaves to go with the flowers, when she heard a shout. She turned and saw a girl about her own age.

'You stop picking those daffodils! How dare you do that!' shouted the girl.

'They're wild ones!' called back Annie. 'Anyone can pick them when the gate to this wood is open.'

'You're a thief!' said the other girl, coming up, looking very angry. 'They're *our* daffodils!'

'But they can't be if this is just a wood,' said Annie. 'And Mark Jones said that if the gate to this wood was open, anyone could come in and pick. *Any*one!'

'Well, you come and tell my mother that silly story and see if she believes you,' said the girl. 'Though I know you won't. I bet you're a nasty little thief and will run out of the gate as soon as I yell for her.'

'I'm *not* a thief!' said Annie indignantly. 'I was *told* I could pick these. I'll certainly come with you and see your mother. I've not been doing anything wrong.'

'All right. You come then,' said the girl, and led Annie through the little wood, up a shady path and then under an archway of yew into a lovely garden. Annie was surprised. Good gracious – perhaps that wood *did* belong to someone then!

Somebody was weeding in the garden. 'Mother!' said the girl, running to her. 'I've caught a daffodil thief. Look at all the flowers she's picked! She's a thief, isn't she?'

'I'm *not*,' said Annie, very cross. 'I tell you Mark Jones *said* anyone could come into the daffodil wood if the gate was open – and it was. I'm very, very sorry if it's *not* a free wood – and please take the daffodils. But I am *not* a thief!'

'She is, Mother, she is, isn't she?' cried the girl.

'Be quiet, Jenny,' said her mother. 'No, I don't think this child *is* a thief. She would have run away if so. Why did you want the daffodils, my dear?'

'Only because my granny's ill,' said Annie. 'I took sixpence out of my moneybox to buy her violets, but Mark said these daffodils were for anyone to pick, if the gate was open.'

'I see,' said Jenny's mother. 'Well, I'll tell you what we'll do. You give me your sixpence, and you can *buy* the daffodils. Then you can give them to your granny.'

'I haven't got the sixpence,' said Annie.

'Oh – but you said you had,' said Jenny's mother.

'She's a fibber, she's a fibber!' said Jenny.

'I am *not*, said Annie fiercely. 'First you call me a thief and now you call me a fibber! I did have a sixpence – but Mark said he would show me the wild daffodils to pick if I'd buy sweets with my sixpence and give him half. So I did. I thought that would be quite fair.'

'Is that the Mark Jones who lives in Dene Street?' asked Jenny's mother. 'And who is your granny?'

'Granny is Mrs Oldfield,' said Annie, 'and Mark does live in Dene Street. But I'm sure he *really* thought the daffodils were wild!'

'I don't think so,' said Jenny's mother. 'This is the third time he has sent people into our wood. He is a very naughty little boy. I know your granny, Annie. She and I have been trying to plan a sale together, you know.'

'Oh, you must be Mrs Harbin then!' cried Annie. 'Well, I expect you know that my granny is ill, if you know her so well.'

'Yes. I heard she was ill only this morning,' said Mrs Harbin. 'And I was going to ask Jenny here to pick some of our daffodils to take to her. But perhaps you will take those you picked yourself to her and say they are from me, with my love – and from you too – will you?'

'Oh, *yes*! Thank you, Mrs Harbin, Granny *will* be delighted!' said Annie. 'And please, you don't think I'm a thief or a fibber, do you? I didn't know it was all a trick of Mark's. Oh, won't I be angry with him tomorrow!'

She said goodbye and went off to Granny's. Oh, that horrid Mark! Tricking her like that! Wouldn't he feel awful when she told him about Mrs Harbin and what she had said?

Her granny was delighted with the daffodils – but Mark was not at all pleased when he heard Annie's tale the next day. He went very red indeed.

'Why did you tell about me? You horrid little sneak!' he said.

'I am *not* a sneak!' said Annie. 'And what's more I'm getting tired of being called all kinds of things that I'm not – a thief, and a fibber – and now a sneak! *I* didn't know you were making it all up about the free daffodils in the wood – it was your own fault for being such a cheat! Getting my toffees for nothing too! You'll be sorry for all this, you see if you won't!'

'Pooh!' said Mark, and walked off. '*I* shan't be sorry. You're the silly one to go and believe all you're told!'

But Mark *was* sorry, because Mrs Harbin and Annie's granny wanted ten children to go and help with their Grand Garden Sale in May, and Mrs Harbin went to ask Annie's teacher if there were ten children in Annie's class that could come and take charge of the donkey rides and the hoopla stalls.

'Well, that's awkward,' said Miss Brown. 'You see, there are *eleven* children in Annie's class. Here's the list. It would be difficult to leave just *one* out.'

Mrs Harbin glanced down the list. She saw Mark's name there, and looked up at once. 'It won't be difficult to know whom to leave out,' she said. 'I don't want Mark Jones to come.'

'Oh dear! What has he done?' asked Miss Brown.

'I don't think I'll tell you that,' said Mrs Harbin. 'But ask Mark if *he* knows why I don't want him. He'll guess, I'm sure!'

Yes. Mark did guess. He won't be at the Great Garden Sale – but he has done something rather surprising. He has left a box of chocolates at Annie's house, bought out of his own money, for Annie to raffle at the sale!

How odd that somebody naughty can do something nice! Annie is very, very pleased.

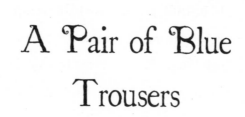

A Pair of Blue
Trousers

A Pair of Blue Trousers

HAVE YOU ever heard people say, 'It will be fine weather today if we can see enough blue sky to make a sailor a pair of trousers?' We often say that, and we look anxiously upwards to see if there is just a little blue patch showing. I wonder if you know how the saying first began?

One year, long ago, there came a terrible spell of cold, cloudy weather. Not a patch of blue sky was to be seen. The weather clerk was in a very bad temper and he wouldn't send even a speck of blue anywhere. People were in despair and couldn't think what to do.

At last they went to a wise woman who lived in her

tumbledown cottage on the very top of Breezy Hill.

'Can you tell us what to do?' they asked. 'We do so badly want good weather.'

The wise woman sat down in her chimney corner and thought for a while. Then she said, 'If you can make the weather clerk put a patch of blue in the sky big enough to make a sailor a pair of trousers, the weather will turn fine again. That is all I can tell you.'

Everyone puzzled over this, and no one could think how to make the weather clerk put a little patch of blue into the heavens. But at last a sailor boy stood up and grinned.

'I'll manage it for you,' he said. 'I've heard that the weather clerk keeps a snappy dog outside his house. I'll pay the clerk a visit and see if his dog will snap a hole in my trousers. Then I'll go in and demand a new pair, and see what I can get out of him.'

So off he went – and you should have heard him growl at the snappy dog, who, of course, growled back and flew at the sailor's trousers. It wasn't long before there was a big hole in them.

The sailor boy marched up to the front door and crashed the knocker down several times. The door flew open and the weather clerk looked out angrily. But before he could speak, the sailor began to shout at the top of his voice, 'Look here, look here! See the hole your dog has made in my trousers. You should have that dog locked up – he is a dangerous animal. You must pay me five pieces of gold for my trousers so that I may get a new pair.'

'Nonsense,' said the clerk, and made as if he would shut the door. But the sailor put his foot in so that he couldn't, and began to shout again.

'Be quiet, pray be quiet,' the clerk begged. 'You are noisier than a thunderstorm. I have no money to give you for a new pair of trousers.'

'Well, I must have a pair!' roared the sailor. 'Give me a bit of blue sky to make myself a new pair. Then I will not charge you anything. Quickly, now, before I fetch the policeman to your dog!'

The weather clerk, shivering and shaking, pulled two clouds apart, and a bit of blue sky peeped between them. The sailor thanked him and ran off in glee.

'Look at the blue sky, look at it!' everyone cried in delight. 'The first we have seen for months!'

'Yes, I got it for you,' said the sailor boy. 'I won't use it for my trousers because you need it for good weather. But please buy me a new pair!'

So they did; and now, on a cloudy day, look up into the sky and see if you can spy a bit of blue big enough to make a sailor a pair of trousers. If you can, you'll see good weather before long.

Eggs and Marbles

Eggs and Marbles

JACK AND Jim were twins and they did everything together. They went to school together, played games together, ran races together, played marbles and went bird nesting with one another.

Their mother didn't mind anything they did except that she hated them to take the eggs out of the birds' nests.

'It makes the birds so sad,' she said. 'It is so unkind of you, Jack and Jim. You don't want the eggs. You don't collect them. You just find the nest, see the eggs and take them. It isn't fair of you. Let the birds have them – they don't belong to you, they belong to the birds.'

But Jack and Jim went on taking the eggs just the same. Their mother found the bright blue eggs belonging to the hedge sparrow on the mantelpiece of the boys' bedroom. She was sad, because she loved the neat little brown hedge sparrows that came about the garden in the winter.

'If you keep taking the eggs, we shall soon have no birds,' she said. 'Now listen – I will give you some beautiful glass marbles, if you will promise me not to take any more eggs.'

The boys loved playing marbles. They promised at once that they would take no more eggs. Their mother took them to a toy shop and bought them eight of the loveliest marbles you can imagine. They were very large, made of glass, and inside the glass were patterns of blue, red and yellow, curving like snakes. Jack and Jim were really delighted.

'Oh, Mother! Aren't they simply beautiful!' said Jack. 'The other children *will* think we are lucky to have these! They will be our very best marbles.'

The two boys were very proud indeed of the wonderful marbles. They showed them to the other children, who tried to make the twins exchange them for sweets, chocolates or toys – but Jack and Jim wouldn't.

'No,' said Jack. 'They are the best marbles in the world. We shall never part with them. We shall keep them till we are grown up, and even then we won't give them away.'

The twins kept their word to their mother for a while, and did not take a single egg. Then, coming home from school one day, Jack saw a robin fly up from the ditch nearby.

'I bet there's a nest there,' he said, and he began to look. Sure enough, there *was* a nest, made of moss and dead leaves. In the nest were three pretty red-brown eggs.

'Robin's eggs,' said Jack. 'Let's take them.'

'We said we wouldn't,' said Jim. 'Look out – there's

the robin come back. Hallo – it's angry!'

The little hen robin was indeed angry. The twins had robbed her first nest of eggs, and her second one as well. Now she had laid three more eggs in this nest, and she wanted to hatch them and have the joy of seeing tiny nestlings cuddled in the cosy nest.

She flew right into Jack's face, and then flapped round Jim's head. The boys laughed. 'Silly little thing! As if *you* could stop us taking your eggs! We'll take them just to spite you.'

The two boys took the three little warm eggs from the nest. The robin was broken-hearted. She flew angrily round their heads, making such a noise that two big jackdaws flying overhead came down to see what the matter was.

They found the little robin sitting on the edge of her nest. Her heart was filled with sadness. Her third batch of eggs was gone. It wasn't any good laying any more. She would have no little ones to feed and love that summer.

The jackdaws listened to all she sang to them. 'It's time we did something to stop those boys from robbing our nests,' said the first jackdaw. 'Do boys have eggs of their own? Shall we go and steal *their* eggs?'

The robin didn't know anything about boys, except that they stole eggs from her nest and from the nests of other birds. 'I wish you *would* steal their eggs, if they have any,' she sang in her creamy voice. 'I wish you would!'

The jackdaws flew off. They saw the house the boys went into. They flew down to the roof. Then they heard the voices of the boys in the bedroom below.

'We'd better hide these robin eggs. Mother would be very upset if she saw them. After all, we did promise we wouldn't take any more.'

The jackdaws waited until they could no longer hear voices, and then they flew down to the windowsill of the bedroom. No one was there. They flew into the room, and walked about the floor, looking for any eggs that might belong to the boys.

'Look!' said the first jackdaw suddenly. 'Eggs! Large, round eggs, all bright and shining.'

The other jackdaw looked. In a box, arranged on cotton wool, were the eight beautiful glass marbles belonging to the boys. The big birds had no idea they were playthings. To them they seemed like big round eggs.

'These are the eggs belonging to the two boys,' clacked the first jackdaw. 'See the nest of wool they are in! We will take all the eggs away. Then they will not hatch and the boys will know what it is to feel unhappy.'

So, one by one, the jackdaws carried away the big glass marbles. They took them to their own enormous nest of sticks, high up in the church tower. There they put the eight wonderful marbles.

The twins came upstairs just as the jackdaws flew out of the window with the last two marbles in their beaks. They gave a scream.

'Our marbles! Mother, Mother, quick! The jackdaws have taken our marbles. They're all gone! Mother, Mother!'

Their mother came running in. She looked at the empty box.

'Poor Jack, poor Jim!' she said. 'You know, jackdaws love bright, shiny things. They must have come along and seen your marbles, and taken them off. They once took a silver thimble of mine.'

'No, Mother, no, they didn't take our marbles because they like shiny things,' sobbed Jack, so upset that he couldn't help owning up to his mother. 'We broke our promise to you – we took some robin eggs – there they are, look, in this drawer – and I'm sure the jackdaws have come along and taken our marbles to punish us! We saw two flying overhead when we stole the robin eggs.'

Mother looked shocked and sad. 'To take eggs is horrid – but to break your word to me when I trusted you is dreadful,' she said. 'To think that my own two

187

little boys should do that, when they love me and I love them!'

She didn't say any more. She went downstairs by herself. The boys were dreadfully upset, because they really did love their mother. They rushed after her to comfort her.

'We'll never do it again!'

'You can trust us, you can really!'

'We're awfully sorry. Forgive us and give us another chance, Mother. Don't look like that!'

'Of course I'll forgive you and give you another chance,' said their mother. 'But I'm afraid you've lost your marbles.'

They had. They are in the nest of the jackdaws, high up in the church tower – but they haven't hatched yet!

A Dreadful Mistake

A Dreadful Mistake

THE CHILDREN were all going home after school, shouting and laughing, and chasing one another. Hilda, who was head of her form, ran with her younger brother Pat to catch the bus.

Just as she leapt on, something flew out of her satchel. It was a sheet of paper, but she didn't see it. Nor did Pat – but someone else did.

Freda saw it, and so did Tom, her brother. Tom ran to pick it up before the bus went, meaning to give it to Hilda, but the bus rumbled off quickly and he couldn't catch it up.

'Don't bother to give it to Hilda,' called Freda.

'Give it to me, Tom.'

'But it's the homework for tomorrow,' said Tom. 'She won't know what work to do tonight when she gets home – and she'll lose all her marks for it. You know how cross Miss Brown is when anyone says they couldn't do their homework because they hadn't their notes.'

'Well, never *mind*,' said Freda. '*I* shall be jolly glad if that swanky Hilda, always top of the form, loses a few marks!'

'She doesn't swank,' said Tom. 'She just works hard. Come on – the bus has gone. We can't do anything about it now!'

He screwed up the sheet of paper and put it into his pocket, meaning to keep it, so that if Miss Brown didn't believe that Hilda had lost the homework notes, he could pull it out and say he had seen it blow out of her satchel. He liked Hilda. She was always fair and generous.

Freda walked home with Tom, pleased that Hilda

would get into trouble the next day. She determined to do her own homework very, very well that evening – and perhaps, if Hilda's homework was not done, she, Freda, might be top in marks for a change! That would show Hilda!

She got out her books that evening very soon after tea, much to everyone's surprise.

'Aren't you going to watch television?' asked Tom, astonished. Nobody could ever get Freda away from the television set in the evenings – and that was one reason why her homework was so poor! She hurried over it each time.

'I've got a lot of work to do,' she announced. 'Please don't interrupt me, anyone!'

She looked for her homework notes. They were not among her books. She scrabbled in her satchel for them. They weren't there either! Blow! Oh, *blow*! She must have left the sheet of notes in the cloakroom on the bench!

'What's the matter?' asked Tom.

'I've left my homework notes on the bench in the cloakroom!' said Freda almost in tears. 'And I can't remember a single thing we had to do!'

'Oh, Freda! That *is* careless!' said her mother. 'That means no marks. Daddy is really getting very cross about your low place in form, you know.'

'There was a poem to learn,' said Freda, 'but I forget which one it was. And sums to do. And an essay to write. Oh *why* did I leave the notes behind? I badly want to do my homework well tonight.'

Tom looked up. 'Well, use these,' he said, and pulled the sheet of notes out of his pocket. He straightened out the paper. 'Don't you remember? Hilda dropped these just as she got on the bus.'

'Thank goodness you kept them!' said Freda joyfully, and took them at once. Soon she was buried in her homework. She looked up the sums in her book and copied them out neatly and did them. She was sure they were all correct.

Then she learnt the little poem very quickly, for

she had a good memory.

Then she wrote the essay. The title was to be 'A Ride on a Bus' and that was easy to Freda for she very often went to visit her granny on a bus.

Her father came in when she had almost finished. 'Done your homework properly?' he asked. 'Let's see your sums.' He looked at them, and then smiled. 'Why, they're all correct!'

'And I had to learn a poem, Daddy – listen,' said Freda, and recited it without a mistake. 'And here's my composition – "A Ride on a Bus".'

Her father read it. 'Well, how is it you are not top of your form if you can do work like this?' he said.

'It's because she likes to watch television so much,' said her mother. 'She says she can do her work *and* watch television – but nobody can, of course.'

'Well, let me know tomorrow night how many marks you get for this,' said her father. 'You should get the full total!'

Freda felt very pleased. Aha – tomorrow would

see her with top marks and Hilda with no marks at all!

Tomorrow came, and the class sat before Miss Brown as usual. Freda was very anxious to give in her work. She could hardly sit still. Tom wasn't in her class, so he wouldn't hear her wonderful marks. He was in the class below with Hilda's brother and did different homework.

All the homework sums were handed in, and the essays too. Freda was astonished to see Hilda handing in her books as well. How *could* she have done any homework if she had lost the notes?

Miss Brown set the class to draw a map, while she corrected the homework. Then she looked up. 'I will give you the marks for the sums,' she said, and read them out.

Freda's name came last – with *no* marks at all! She stared in amazement. Then Miss Brown gave the marks for the essays – and again Freda had none at all! She went very red and longed to ask why. But she didn't like to. Something must have gone very, very wrong!

'Now I'll hear the little poem you learnt for me last night,' said Miss Brown. 'Stand up, Jane, and say it first.'

Jane wasn't very good at saying poetry, but she got on quite well – and Freda sat listening in amazement. Surely Jane wasn't saying the right poem? It wasn't the one that she, Freda, had learnt! She listened to all the others saying the same poem, one by one. At last it came to her turn.

She wondered if she could remember the poem she had been listening to. She tried to say it, stumbling over the lines till Miss Brown stopped her.

'That's enough, Freda. You didn't learn the poem at all, did you?'

'No, Miss Brown,' said Freda, 'I – I learnt another one.'

'But why?' asked Miss Brown. 'And why did you hand in wrong sums and write an essay about "A Ride on a Bus", when I told you all yesterday to write one on "A Dog I Have Known"? Didn't you write down what you had to do for homework?'

'Yes, Miss Brown – but I forgot to take it home,' said Freda.

'But why give in *wrong* homework? Did you think I wouldn't notice that it was the same homework I gave you all to do a *month ago*?' asked Miss Brown. 'I think you are being very silly, Freda. You have no marks at all today.'

'Freda was away ill a month ago,' said Hilda. 'She didn't do that homework then, Miss Brown – how can she have done it *yesterday* then? She couldn't have had the notes for it!'

'Can you explain, please, Freda?' asked Miss Brown, frowning.

'Well – some notes blew out of Hilda's bag yesterday,' said Freda. 'And my brother picked them up. And when I got home I found I'd left my own homework notes behind, so I used Hilda's – but I didn't know they were a month old. I'm – I'm very sorry, Miss Brown.'

'It's a very strange thing that you got *all* the sums right and did a good essay for once in a way,' said Miss Brown. 'Can you explain why *that* is, Freda?'

Freda could have explained, of course. She *could* have said that she had thought they really *were* yesterday's homework notes and, because she felt that Hilda wouldn't be able to do *her* homework at all, she, Freda, had decided for once to work hard, and be top! But she wasn't going to say all that. She was in enough disgrace as it was!

And then that night she had to face her father's questions too. 'Well, Freda – I suppose you were top of the class today!' he said, when he came in. 'Tell me the good news! Was your essay the best?'

'No, Daddy,' said Freda, not looking at him. 'Hilda was top again.'

'Oh. Well, what about your poem? You must have had top marks for that,' said her father, disappointed.

'You were quite word perfect.'

'Well – unluckily I – I learnt the *wrong* poem!' said Freda desperately.

'The *wrong* poem! How could you be so careless as to do that?' said her father, annoyed. 'Don't tell me you did the wrong sums too!'

'Yes, I did,' said Freda, with tears in her eyes. 'It was a dreadful mistake, Daddy. I left my homework notes at school – and worked from some old ones of Hilda's – and – well – I got no marks at all.'

'I see,' said her father gravely. 'What's the matter with you, Freda? You get bad marks nearly always for doing the *right* work – and yet, as I saw myself, you did splendid work last night – really splendid – but you were so careless that it was the *wrong* work! Is there any chance of your doing the *right* work really well each night?'

'Yes, Daddy,' said Freda.

'Well, no watching of television until you show me that you can,' said Daddy. 'Remember – you did that good work yesterday when the television was *off*. You've got to earn your television programmes, Freda. Do you understand?'

Freda understood! Daddy never went back on his word, and now that he knew she *could* work hard, she would have to – or never watch television again.

She's had top marks for one week, and has been second in form twice. And now she's beginning to wonder if it wasn't a good thing that Hilda lost her wrong homework notes that day, and Tom picked them up!

'I've such good brains – as good as Hilda's – and I suppose it's a shame not to use them!' she says. Well, I rather think you're right, Freda!

Funny-One's Present

Funny-One's Present

'IT'S MOTHER Kindly's birthday at the end of October,' said Pippity. 'We all ought to give her a present. She's so kind.'

'Yes, we ought,' said Jinks. 'I shall see how much I've got in my moneybox. I shall buy her a very grand present.'

'I shall make her something,' said Winky. 'I think I shall sew her a cushion for her back. She's old and she gets tired now.'

Mother Kindly didn't know that all her friends were planning birthday presents for her. She was an old woman, with bright eyes and a kind smile. She had been kind to every single person in the village. There wasn't anyone she hadn't visited when they were ill. She remembered all their birthdays. She lent them money when they had none, and she did their shopping for them when they were too busy.

But she hadn't had a very happy life. Once her little cottage had been burnt down and she had lost everything. Then her daughter, Golden Hair, had run away with a horrid goblin, and he had never let her come back once to see her mother.

Another time all her hens had died of a mysterious illness, and in one sad week Growler, her dog, had been harmed and Bunty, her cat, had been caught in a trap.

'She's never had a year full of happiness,' said Funny-One, thinking hard. 'Never. Even last year the cows got into her garden and ate all the vegetables she had grown so carefully. And somebody got in and stole all her best clothes. I wish I could give her good luck as a present.'

'Well, you can buy a piece of good luck from Witch Glinty,' said Jinks. 'But it costs a terrible lot.'

'I haven't any money at all,' said Funny-One. 'So it's no good my going to buy good luck. I wish I could think of something else.'

It was Silver Tip who gave him an idea. 'Do you know,' she said, 'that every falling leaf you catch while it's still in the air means a happy day for you next year? Did you know that, Funny-One?'

'No, I didn't,' said Funny-One. 'Does it really?'

'Well, that's what everyone says,' said Silver Tip, and danced off, leaving Funny-One thinking very hard.

Now, it was autumn then, and the October leaves were beginning to whirl down in the wind. Funny-One saw them fluttering in the air.

He spent a long time dancing about trying to catch leaves. He caught three off the poplar tree.

He looked at them. 'You mean three happy days next year,' he said. 'If I had three hundred and sixty-five of you, I'd be certain of a whole year of happiness.' Then he had the Grand Idea. 'And if I gave you to Mother Kindly, *she* would have a happy year – a happy year for the first time, I should think, with no bad luck or disappointments in it. How pleased she would be!'

Well, no sooner had he thought of this than he knew what his birthday present to Mother Kindly was going to be! It was going to be a sack with three hundred and sixty-five leaves in it, that he had caught in mid-air! Fancy being able to give somebody a whole year of happiness. Funny-One was very pleased.

His friends laughed at him in the next days, for they saw him dancing and capering in the woods, trying to catch leaves that would most annoyingly flutter away just as he had almost got them.

'I've got fifty-three,' he panted, stuffing one into his sack. 'I'll have to hurry if I'm going to get the right number – over three hundred more.'

At last the day before Mother Kindly's birthday

came, and when Funny-One carefully counted his leaves he found that he still needed twenty-four more. So out he went into the moonlit night and caught leaf after leaf in the frosty air. And at last he had twenty-four, and when he added them to the others, they came to three hundred and sixty-five.

Mother Kindly saw Funny-One capering about in the moonlight and she was astonished. *Silly little Funny-One!* she thought. *What is he doing?*

Next morning all the little villagers went along to Mother Kindly's house with their birthday presents.

'A happy birthday to you! Here's a cushion I have made!'

'Many happy returns of the day! Here's a dozen new-laid eggs!'

'Happy birthday! Here's a new clock that chimes every half-hour!'

'Lots of happy birthdays to you! Here's a shawl I've knitted all myself.'

'Oh, Mother Kindly! I've come to wish you a

very happy birthday, and here's my present for you!' panted Funny-One, coming in with a big sack. How everyone stared! -

'What's in the sack, Funny-One?' asked Winky.

'A whole happy year!' said Funny-One. 'I caught it for Mother Kindly.'

Winky opened the sack and saw a heap of dead leaves there. He laughed. 'Pooh! Just a lot of dead leaves! There's no Happy Year here.'

But Mother Kindly took Funny-One's hand and she kissed him. 'Funny-One, it's a lovely present. I know the old saying about every falling leaf that is caught will bring a happy day next year, and I expect, you funny little one, that you have caught three hundred and sixty-five!'

'Yes, I did,' said Funny-One. 'So now you'll have a year without any bad luck or unhappiness, Mother Kindly.'

'You're a dear little person,' said Mother Kindly. 'Most people would have kept the Happy Year for themselves. But you have brought it to me. It's my Very Nicest Present!'

Funny-One was delighted. He went home feeling very warm and happy. It was nice to give a Happy Year to somebody he loved.

And will you believe, Mother Kindly had a perfectly wonderful year of happiness, without one single day of bad luck or disappointment. She didn't even have a toothache or cut her finger. It was marvellous.

So it does look as if there's something in that old saying, doesn't it? I think I shall catch a few leaves myself for somebody I love. I'd like to think they'd have some happy days because of me!

Donald's Trees

Donald's Trees

MISS BROWN wanted her class to grow some fine bulbs in her bowls, and she wanted each child to take a bulb home too, and grow it in their bedroom, so that they might watch it for themselves.

'Ask your mothers if they can spare us some pennies to buy bulbs with,' said Miss Brown. 'I will bring the bowls and buy the fibre.'

Every child but Donald brought a penny or two. But Donald's mother couldn't spare even a ha'penny! So poor Donald didn't go to buy any bulbs, and there wasn't one for him to take home to grow.

'You must share the school ones,' said Miss Brown.

'Now, children, listen. Take care of your bulbs at home, and in the New Year, when they are in bloom, we will have a bulb show, and there will be a prize for the best grown!'

So each child tended their own bulb at home very carefully, and hoped it would grow well. Only Donald had no bulb, and when all the other children told Miss Brown how their plants were getting on, he had nothing to say.

But Donald was not going to have nothing at all to grow! No, he wasn't that sort of boy! If he couldn't have a bulb, he would have something else. So he saved a nice brown pip out of a ripe apple, and he took a pip from an orange. He went walking in the woods and found a fat acorn and a round polished conker. He took them home. Then he went to the flower shop round the corner, and asked the kind old woman there a question. 'Please, have you one or two little broken flowerpots to spare? I want to grow something.'

The old lady gave him four tiny ones that had had

small heather plants in. Donald washed them, put some little stones at the bottom, over the hole, and then filled them with earth. He planted an apple pip in one, an orange pip in another, the acorn in the third and the conker in the last pot. He set them on the windowsill in the winter sunshine. He kept them watered and he looked at the pots a great deal.

Well, after a time, from each pot came a small green shoot! The conker and the acorn were the biggest. It was fun watching them grow. Donald didn't say a word to the other children, for he was afraid of being laughed at – and it isn't nice to be laughed at, is it?

After the New Year, Miss Brown began to think about the bulb show. 'You had better all bring your bulbs next week,' she said. 'But what about you, Donald? You didn't have anything to grow, did you?'

'No, I didn't, Miss Brown,' said Donald. 'I *am* growing something – but not bulbs! I'm growing an apple tree, an orange tree, an oak tree and a chestnut tree – all in my bedroom!'

Well, of course, that astonished everyone very much, and Miss Brown said Donald really *must* bring his plants to school too. So he did, and they were put on the windowsill with the bulbs. All the children loved the little trees, and Donald went red with delight.

'You meant to grow *some*thing!' said Miss Brown with a laugh. 'Well, there are two prizes – and one shall go to Winnie's beautful pink hyacinth – and the other shall go to your little trees, Donald!'

'Oh, thank you!' said Donald, as he took the book of stories. 'Miss Brown, when my apple tree is grown, I will sell the apples, and buy bulbs for everyone in the school!'

Won't he feel grand when he does?

One Saturday Morning

One Saturday Morning

EVERY SATURDAY Sally and Bill had a shilling each to spend. Sometimes they spent it at the toy shop, sometimes at the sweet shop. It was great fun deciding what to buy.

'I know what I'm going to buy today,' said Bill one Saturday morning. 'A whip for my top! I keep making silly little whips out of sticks and string, but what I want is a *proper* whip, with cord to make the top spin for ages and ages.'

'Yes. It's such a nice top,' said Sally, looking at the fine, carved top in Bill's hand. 'Grandpa made it for you, didn't he, and carved it too. I'll come with you to buy the whip. I'm going to the toy shop too.'

They went off together, each with their own shilling. 'What are *you* going to buy?' asked Bill.

'Well, you know Tiddler, that small new doll of mine, don't you?' said Sally. 'The toy shop has a whole lot of small dolls' dresses in, and I'm going to buy one for Tiddler. She only has an overall I made her, and it's not very nice.'

'We shan't have much left for sweets today,' said Bill. 'Those whips are ninepence!'

They went into the toy shop and looked round. It was a lovely place – the kind of place they would have liked to spend all morning in! But so many children went there on Saturdays that Miss Dorrit, whose shop it was, shooed them out once they had been served.

'Now, now – how can I see what I'm doing if all the children in the village crowd into my shop on Saturday mornings!' she said. 'Well, Bill, what do you want?'

'One of those top-whips,' said Bill, pointing. 'You

said last week they were very good.'

'So they are,' said Miss Dorrit. 'Jack Lane told me he kept his top going for twenty-one minutes last week, with one of those cord-whips! Choose which you like, Bill. They're ninepence each.'

'And I want one of those little dolls' dresses,' said Sally. 'May I have that blue one, please. It's for the little new doll I bought last Saturday.'[

'Ah – this will fit her well,' said Miss Dorrit, and wrapped it up for her. Then Bill came up with his whip he had chosen, and the two children paid Miss Dorrit their money – ninepence for the whip, and ninepence for the little dress.

'And now you've got threepence each to spend on chocolate,' she said, smiling. She knew what every child in the village had to spend each Saturday!

They went home, Bill longing to spin his top, and Sally longing to dress her new little doll. But as soon as they were in their playroom, one of their sudden quarrels blew up!

'Have you moved my top?' said Bill loudly, looking round for it. 'I left it here, on the floor. Where have you put it, Sally? I've *told* you not to move my things!'

'I haven't *touched* it!' said Sally. 'And don't shout at me like that.'

'I'm *not* shouting,' said Bill, raising his voice a little more. 'I'm just asking you politely where my top is!'

'You're *not* asking me politely,' snapped Sally, beginning to shout too. 'And just take your whip off my doll's cot. You'll be saying I've put *that* somewhere in a minute.'

Bill took no notice, but went on looking for his top, crawling about on the floor.

'Didn't you hear me tell you to take your whip off Tiddler's cot?' demanded Sally. 'All right – if you won't move it, *I* will!'

And she picked it up and threw it at Bill. It bounced off his shoulder – and shot straight into the fire! Bill gave a howl and dashed to get it out.

But the fire was a big blazing one, and before he could get the whip, the cord had perished in the flames. Bill held the scorched handle and looked in dismay at the burnt cord.

'You horrid girl!' he said, in a real rage. 'You nasty, horrid, bad-tempered girl! I'll pay you out for that!'

And before Sally could even say she was sorry, he snatched up the new little dress she was just going to put on her doll and tore it to rags!

Mother came in when she heard Sally's loud crying and Bill's shouts. 'She threw my whip into the fire, my new whip, and it cost ninepence!' shouted Bill. 'And she's taken my top, I know she has!'

'No, she hasn't,' said Mother, and took it down from the mantelpiece. 'You left it on the floor again, Bill, and I stepped on it and almost ricked my ankle. So *I* took it and put it safely up here.'

'Mother, he tore my new doll's frock to pieces, look!' wept Sally. 'And I only bought it this morning.'

'I'm ashamed of you both,' said Mother in disgust.

'All the money you spent has been wasted because of your bad tempers.' She went out of the room and shut the door.

Sally and Bill turned their backs on one another. They were already ashamed of being so silly and unkind. Why, oh why, did they lose their tempers so quickly? They said nothing at all to one another, but Bill could hear Sally giving little sniffs now and again as if she was still crying over her torn doll's frock. He peeped at her out of the corner of his eye.

She was trying to mend the torn frock and not making a very good job of it. Bill loved his small sister and was suddenly very sorry. She had been so pleased with that frock for her new little doll. How *could* he have torn it to bits!

After a while Sally took a look at what Bill was doing. He was sitting, quite silent, trying to tie a piece of ordinary string on to his new whip, which, scorched and without cord, looked a poor thing now. Then it was Sally's turn to feel sad. She knew better than anyone how pleased Bill had been to buy a whip worthy of his fine top.

Soon Bill got up and went out. He was away quite a long time, and then Sally saw him coming in at the gate. She wondered where he had been. As he came in, she went out, and she too was gone quite a long time. It was dinnertime before she came back. Mother called to them.

'Come and have your dinner, children. I hope you've got over your bad tempers by now!'

Sally walked into the dining room. Bill was there waiting for her. As soon as she got to her seat, he pushed something into her hand.

'Here! I've got this for you. I'm sorry I tore the other dress to bits, Sally,' he said. And lo and behold, Sally found herself holding a dear little doll's dress, almost like the one she had chosen that morning. She stared at Bill in surprise.

'Oh, *Bill*!' she said. 'I'm sorry too – and here is something for *you*!' She pushed a parcel into his hand,

and he undid it. It was a whip with a cord, just like the one that had been burnt in the fire!

'*Well!*' said Mother, very pleased. 'I *am* glad you've both been kind, and made up to one another for the silly things you did. But where did you get the money from to go and buy them, children?'

'Oh, Mother!' said Sally. 'Oh, *Mother*! I took my new little doll that I bought last Saturday back to the toy shop, and Miss Dorrit changed it for a new whip!'

'And I took my lovely top and changed it at the toy shop for a new doll's dress!' said Bill. 'Miss Dorrit said she would let me just for once.'

'I see,' said Mother. And then she began to laugh. 'Oh, you two dear, silly children!' she said. '*You* have brought Sally a doll's frock, Bill – but now she hasn't a doll to put it on! She has given it in exchange for that whip – but *you* don't need a whip now because you haven't a top to spin! You exchanged it for the dress! What *am* I to do with children like you?'

'I don't know,' said Bill and Sally together, looking

surprised, but much happier now.

'We'll have to wait till next Saturday and then buy my doll back and Bill's top, when we have our next shillings,' said Sally.

But they won't have to wait! Mother's gone down to the toy shop herself. She'll be back in a short while, and I'm sure you can guess what there will be in her basket!

The Boy Who Didn't Believe

The Boy Who Didn't Believe

THERE WAS once a little boy called Jim who didn't believe in fairies. The fairies didn't mind at all, and really never thought about him. But the gnomes, who sometimes hid themselves in his garden, grew very angry when they heard him one day singing a song he had made up himself:

'There aren't any gnomes or fairies,
Or witches or giants tall;
There are not any goblins or pixies,
There's nothing like that at all!'

That was what Jim sang as he wandered round his garden.

'Silly little boy!' snorted the gnomes who were listening. 'Let's punish him for making up such a horrid song!'

'Yes, let's,' said the leader. 'And I know how – let's put him into Fairyland, and tell him to find his way home! He'll keep meeting people he doesn't believe in, and he *will* get such a shock!'

All the gnomes thought it would be a splendid idea, and when Jim came near them they threw themselves on him, blindfolded his eyes, and led him straight into Fairyland.

'Oh, oh! Let me go, let me go!' cried Jim, very frightened.

'*We'll* let you go!' chuckled the gnomes, as they took away the handkerchief from his eyes.

'Where am I?' asked Jim, looking around; but the gnomes had vanished, and he was quite alone.

'What a funny thing!' said Jim to himself. 'Whoever

did that to me? And wherever am I?'

He was standing in the middle of a field which was full of the loveliest flowers he had ever seen. By him was a signpost on which was painted:

THIS WAY TO THE WISHING WELL

'Well, I may as well go along to the wishing well,' decided Jim, 'and perhaps I shall find out the way home.'

He followed a little winding path across the field until he came to a stile. To his surprise there was a large yellow bird on the top. It perched there and looked at him, without attempting to fly away.

'You lovely tame thing!' said Jim, stroking its shiny feathers. 'But how am I to get over the stile, I wonder, with you sitting on top?'

'Why didn't you say you wanted to get over?' asked the bird, flying into the hedge nearby.

Jim nearly jumped out of his skin! He looked at

the bird as if he couldn't believe his eyes.

'What are you staring at me like that for?' asked the yellow bird in an angry voice.

'My goodness!' exclaimed Jim, finding his tongue again. 'Well! Goodness gracious! Whoever heard of a bird talking like that before?'

'Don't be silly,' said the yellow bird, 'you know you're in Fairyland, where all the birds can talk!'

'In Fairyland!' cried Jim. 'But I can't be, there isn't such a place!'

'You *are* a silly boy!' remarked the bird crossly. 'Fancy saying there isn't such a place when you're there all the time!'

'Well, I *don't* believe in Fairyland. Would you please tell me the way home?'

But the yellow bird only snorted at him in disgust, and flew away over the field.

This is *a funny place, and no mistake!* thought Jim, climbing over the stile into the next field.

In the middle of the field was a funny,

higgledy-piggledy well, and sitting on the wall round it was a pretty little fairy dressed in mauve.

Jim rubbed his eyes and pinched himself.

'It *can't* be a fairy!' he said. 'It simply can't! It must be somebody dressed up like one.'

He ran up to the well. 'What are you dressed up like a fairy for?' he asked the little mauve fairy.

She looked puzzled. 'I *am* a fairy,' she answered.

'But there aren't any fairies!' said Jim. 'So you can't be one.'

'You're a silly little boy,' said the fairy rather crossly. 'You're in Fairyland, where there are *lots* of fairies!'

'Well, I *don't* believe in fairies,' said Jim, 'and I'll sing you the little song I made up about them.'

Jim began singing: '*There aren't any gnomes or fairies—*'

'Hush! Hush!' cried the mauve fairy. 'You mustn't sing things like that here! You'll have the Lord High Chamberlain of Fairyland after you, and he'll turn you into a frog or something.'

Jim stopped and looked rather frightened. Then he saw someone clambering over the stile in the distance, waving a stick and shouting.

'Oh, dear! Is that the Lord High Chamberlain?' he asked.

'Yes, it is! Oh, goodness me, how can I save you! He looks terribly angry!' cried the mauve fairy.

Jim was so frightened that, without thinking what he was doing, he jumped straight into the wishing well! He fell down and down and down, until at last, splash! He was in water up to his waist.

'Where's that boy gone?' he heard the chamberlain roaring. '*I'll* teach him to sing songs like that in Fairyland! I'll teach him!'

After a little while Jim saw the mauve fairy leaning over the top of the well.

'He's gone!' she called. 'But he and the yellow bird are looking for you all over the place.'

'Whatever shall I do?' asked poor Jim.

'Well, there's only one thing left for you to do; you

must go and ask the queen to forgive you and let you go home,' said the mauve fairy.

'How can I get to her?' asked Jim.

'Let me think. You can't come up here again, for the yellow bird will see you. You must go through the underground passages till you come to the rushing lift,' advised the fairy. 'Anyone will tell you the way from there. You'll find a little door let into the well wall if you climb up a few steps.'

Jim found the steps, climbed up a little way and discovered a door.

'I've found it,' he called. 'Thank you very much for helping me.'

'Goodbye!' cried the fairy, waving to him.

Jim opened the door, and found himself in a narrow passage, lit by one large lantern hung on a nail. He took it down to carry with him.

He went for a good way and eventually he came to a door.

'It sounds as if there's someone crying inside

there!' said Jim, listening.

He pushed open the door and looked in. Sitting on a stool was a little gnome, sobbing as if his heart would break.

'What's the matter?' asked Jim in a kind voice.

'Oh, dear!' sobbed the gnome. 'My lamp has gone out and I can't finish my work, and it *must* be done this evening.'

'Well, have my lantern,' said Jim, feeling sorry for the little gnome.

'Oh, can you spare it? Thank you so much!' cried the gnome happily. 'Now I can finish my work!'

Jim went out of the room, into the dark passage again, and this time he had to *feel* his way about, for he had no lantern. He was rather frightened, but he tried to pretend he wasn't.

At last he came into a well-lit passage where a lot of animals hurried to and fro. There were rabbits, hedgehogs, moles and hares, and they all looked very busy.

'Where are you going?' Jim asked a grey rabbit, who was dragging a very large sack.

'To market!' panted the rabbit. 'It's market day in Oak Tree Town today. Oh, dear! This sack *is* so heavy.'

'I'll help you,' said Jim, and put the heavy sack on his shoulder, while the rabbit ran beside him.

Presently they came to a big purple chair.

'This is the rushing lift,' explained the rabbit, sitting down on the chair.

'Good! I want to go up in it!' exclaimed Jim and sat down beside the rabbit.

Whiz-z-z-z! Whoosh! Up went the chair at such a tremendous pace that Jim could hardly breathe.

At the top was a large garden and nearby a great palace.

'That's the queen's palace,' said the grey rabbit, 'and oh my goodness! Here's the queen herself in the garden!'

Jim saw a tall and beautiful lady with great blue

wings standing near him. He went up to her and knelt down on one knee.

'Please, Your Majesty,' he said, 'I'm the boy who sang that horrid song, and will you forgive me, because I'm sorry?'

Suddenly the Lord High Chamberlain rushed up, and the yellow bird flew down.

'No, *don't* forgive him, Your Majesty. He doesn't believe in fairies! He's a horrid boy!' they cried.

'He's a *kind* boy,' cried the grey rabbit, 'he carried my heavy sack.'

'Yes,' said another voice, 'and he lent me his lantern to see by when my lamp went out.' It was the little gnome Jim had heard crying. He had suddenly appeared from somewhere with Jim's lantern.

'Do you believe in fairies?' asked the queen gently.

'Oh *yes*, I do now!' cried Jim. 'And I'm sorry I've been so silly and horrid. Please don't let the chamberlain punish me!'

'Well, he was going to,' said the queen, 'but as I

hear you've been so kind to two of my people, I'm going to forgive you.'

'Oh, thank you!' cried Jim. 'And may I go home soon?'

The queen waved her wand.

Everything grew mistier and mistier. The queen faded, and the chamberlain ...

Then suddenly everything grew bright again!

'Hurray!' cried Jim. 'I'm in my own garden! And *what* an adventure I've had! I'll *never* say I don't believe in fairies again!'

And you should have heard the gnomes nearby chuckling when they heard that!

A Real Bit of Luck!

A Real Bit of Luck!

'THE JACKDAWS are building in the chimney of the old ruined tower again,' said Hilda to her older brother Peter. 'Let's go and watch them. It's so funny to see them carrying big twigs in their beaks, and putting them into the great chimney of the tower.'

'All right. I'll come in a minute,' said Peter, shutting his book. 'You go on – I'll catch you up.'

Hilda set off alone. She walked up the slope to where the ruined tower stood up against the sky, watching the jackdaws circling round it, some with twigs in their mouths. One had quite a big stick, which made him fly very clumsily. Hilda laughed as she watched him.

She saw a boy in front of her, and wondered if he was going to watch the amusing jackdaws too. '*Chack-chack-chack!*' they said, just as if they were saying their own name over and over again.

But the boy wasn't going to watch them. No – he had a catapult. He was going to hit them with stones if he could!

Hilda saw the catapult and felt frightened. No! No, surely the boy wouldn't be cruel enough to try and hit the nesting jackdaws! She hurried after him.

'I say! What's the catapult for?' she said.

'I'm going to punish as many jackdaws as I can!' said the boy fiercely. 'I hate them!'

'But why? They haven't done *you* any harm!' said Hilda, horrified.

'Oh, haven't they? Well, one came this morning into my mother's bedroom, and took her lovely necklace off her dressing table!' said the boy angrily.

'And she's very upset about it. So I've come up here to punish those thieving jackdaws!'

'But you don't know which one took the necklace!' cried Hilda. 'You can't punish lots of them just because *one* took the necklace! Besides, the jackdaw only took it because jackdaws always love bright things! He's probably popped it into his nest.'

'Well, what good is that to me?' said the boy. 'I can't climb up there and look into every nest, can I? But I *can* punish those thieving birds!'

He put a stone into his catapult – but Hilda tugged at his arm. 'No! No, you're not to! Look, here comes my brother, I'll get *him* to stop you!'

And Peter certainly did stop him! He snatched at the wicked catapult and put it into his own pocket. 'If you want it back, you'll have to come and get it,' he said. 'But I warn you – I learn boxing, and you won't get the best of any fight.'

The angry boy looked at the determined Peter, who already had his fists up, ready for an attack. Then, to

Hilda's surprise, he suddenly swung aside and ran away! Down the hill he went at top speed!

'Those who like to hurt creatures that can't defend themselves are always cowards!' shouted Peter, throwing down the catapult and stamping on it. 'Come on, Hilda – don't look so scared. Thanks to you, no harm is done. Good thing I came when I did!'

'Yes,' said Hilda, feeling a bit shaky at the knees, very thankful that Peter learnt boxing. 'Come on, let's sit here and watch the jackdaws for a bit – and then we'll go into the tower and collect all the loose twigs that have fallen down the chimney and stack them outside, so that the jackdaws can fly down and use them again.'

They watched the noisy, chattering birds in delight. How they talked! How they scolded one another! How funny it was when two jackdaws collided with their big sticks, and dropped them because they wanted to call each other rude names!

'Now let's go into the tower and pick up the fallen

sticks,' said Hilda and they both went into the dark ruined tower. The floor was scattered with twigs that had fallen down the great chimney. Peter began to pick up an armful, and Hilda did the same.

Suddenly her eye caught sight of something strange, lying in the twig-scattered fireplace at the bottom of the old tower. She bent down to see what it was, and gave an astonished cry.

'Peter! Peter, look! What do you suppose this is?' Peter stopped and looked round, his arms full of twigs. He came over to the fireplace and stared down at it. He saw something shining there among the fallen sticks.

'Push those sticks away and pick it up,' he said. 'I've got my arms full.'

Hilda slid her hand under the fallen twigs and caught hold of the long, shining thing. She pulled it out and held it up.

'Peter! It's a necklace – a lovely, shining necklace – see how it glitters!'

'Goodness – it must be the necklace that boy was telling us about!' said Peter. 'The one that a jackdaw took off his mother's dressing table! Jackdaws love bright things, and I expect one spotted it as he flew past, and went in to get it.'

'And he brought it to his nest here!' cried Hilda. 'I'm sure he did. And it slipped through the loose twigs of his nest up in the tower – and slithered all the way down to the fireplace below. Oh, Peter!'

'Well, that's lucky for that boy's mother,' said Peter. 'Very lucky. We'll be able to take it back to her.'

Hilda slipped the necklace into her pocket and put her hanky on top to prevent it from falling out. 'Hadn't we better go straight back with it?' she said. 'We'll just put these twigs down outside for the jackdaws to use again – and then we'll go back to the town.'

In half a minute they had left the noisy jackdaws hovering round the sticks they had left for them, and were going down the hill. They passed the police station on the way and saw a notice outside.

LOST – A GOLD NECKLACE.
TWO POUNDS REWARD TO
FINDER.

'I wonder if that's the necklace we found!' cried Hilda. 'Two pounds reward! We'd be able to buy a new cage for our budgie! Quick, let's take the necklace into the police station.'

Well, it *was* the lost necklace – and very proudly the children went with a policeman to the owner's house. The horrid boy was in the garden, another catapult in his hand, very surprised to see them. The policeman saw the catapult at once.

'Give that to me!' he said sternly. 'Are you the boy who's been smashing the streetlamps with stones from his catapult? I shall have to report this to your father.'

'I suppose those kids told tales!' said the boy angrily.

'Oh, no – they found your mother's necklace and have come with me to give it back and get the reward,' said the policeman.

'If you had put away your catapult up at the tower and helped us with what we were doing, *you'd* have found the necklace,' said Hilda. 'But instead you wanted to punish birds!'

The boy's mother was delighted to have her necklace back. She heard the children's tale, and then opened her purse. 'Two pounds reward for you!' she said. 'And very glad I am to give it to you! Thank you for finding my necklace!'

They said goodbye and went out again with the policeman. They saw the boy scowling at them from behind a hedge.

'Did you tell my mother about the catapult?' he said.

'No – but we will if we see you with one again!'

said Peter. 'Look – we've got the reward – two pound notes!'

'I wish *I'd* got two pounds!' said the boy, looking longingly at the money.

'Well, you needn't think we're going to share it with you!' said Peter. 'It's come to us simply because we went up to give the jackdaws a hand with their nest building – and it's going to help *another* kind of bird – our budgie!'

You should see the new cage they have bought – it's a real beauty. 'Pretty, pretty, pretty!' says the budgie as he jigs about the perches – and he's quite right – it *is* pretty!

How Very Odd!

How Very Odd!

LITTLE MR Twinkle was out of a job. He had been with Mr Biscuit the Baker for many years – and now Mr Biscuit had sold the shop to a shoemaker and gone away.

The shoemaker didn't want Twinkle. 'You're used to buns and biscuits,' he told Mr Twinkle. 'You're too old to get used to shoes and boots. You'd be weighing them in the scales and selling them at sixpence a pound!'

So here was old Mr Twinkle looking for a new job, with only a sixpence in his pocket, wondering what he was going to do when he had spent it! He wore his old green mackintosh as usual, and hummed a little song as he went, though he didn't really *feel* like humming!

> '*Nowhere to go*
> *And nothing to eat,*
> *Here I come walking*
> *On shuffling feet!*

> '*Nothing to eat*
> *And nowhere to go,*
> *Where shall I sleep,*
> *I really don't know!*'

He made up his funny little song as he went, wondering when he would find another job. He would ask when he got to the next town. Perhaps a baker's shop there would take him on.

He came at last to Cheer-Up Town, and he liked the name very much. He felt so hungry that he thought he really *must* spend his sixpence. What on? A cup of soup and a roll of bread? A big ham sandwich and a glass of water? A boiled egg and bread-and-butter?

'Dear me, I could eat *all* those things!' said Twinkle hungrily. 'Hallo – it's raining. Well, my mac isn't much use now, it's so thin – so I'd better go into a shop and spend my sixpence, and hope the rain will stop.'

He came to a teashop and looked into the window. He saw neat sandwiches there, arranged in piles. Slices of fruit cake. Little meat pies, sausage rolls. Goodness, if only he could have some of each!

The rain fell down in torrents and Mr Twinkle went quickly into the shop. He found that it would be cheapest to have two small ham sandwiches and a glass of water. They would cost him sixpence.

So he sat down and ordered them and paid for them. Then he munched the first sandwich and thought that he had never in his life tasted anything so good. But then he had never in his life felt so hungry before!

The teashop began to get quite full, for people were coming in out of the rain. They sat down at the little tables and ordered all kinds of things: cakes, ice creams, sandwiches, biscuits. Dear me, how rich everyone seemed – even the children!

'Just look at that boy over there – he's got a whole plate of cakes – and he's ordered a double ice cream too!' said Twinkle to himself, and immediately made up another little song.

> '*A plate of cakes,*
> *A double ice cream,*
> *To me it's just*
> *A lovely dream!*
>
> '*And over there,*
> *Good gracious me,*
> *A man has ordered*
> Such *a tea!*
>
> '*Two poached eggs,*
> *A toasted bun,*

HOW VERY ODD!

A slice of cake,
Dear me, what fun!'

'Whatever are you muttering about?' said a cross-looking man at the next table, and Mr Twinkle felt quite ashamed of himself. He got up to go, even though it was still raining, very red in the face. Now – where had he hung his green mackintosh? He went to the row of pegs, unhooked the mackintosh and went out of the teashop.

'I'm off again
On my two feet,
Those sandwiches
Were quite a treat!'

hummed Mr Twinkle as he went along in the rain.

'My feet are wet,
I wish that I

Could catch a bus
And keep them dry!

'If only wishes
Would come true,
What lots of lovely
Things I'd do!'

He went humming down the puddly street, getting very wet indeed. He put his hands into the pockets of his mackintosh to keep them dry, wishing that he still had the little sixpence there. But he had spent it at the teashop.

He felt something in one of the pockets and took it out in surprise. What an extraordinary thing – it was a little leather purse! Twinkle stared at it and his heart began to beat fast.

'My word – is there a bit of magic about today? I wished I could ride in a bus – and now here's a purse of money and I *can* ride in one if I want to!'

He opened the purse. There wasn't a *great* deal of money in it – but still there was half-a-crown, a shilling, two sixpences and three pennies. That seemed riches to Mr Twinkle who hadn't even a ha'penny!

> *'A magic purse!*
> *Hip, hip, hurray,*
> *This really is*
> *My lucky day!'*

sang Mr Twinkle. 'Now let me see – what shall I do with all this money? First I'll find somewhere to sleep tonight and see how much it will cost. Then I will buy some food for my supper. And I will be sure to leave a shilling over for tomorrow, just in case the purse has no money in it then. Though, of course, if it's a magic purse, it may fill itself again!'

> *'Would anyone think*
> *I'd find a purse*

When things had gone
From bad to worse!'

Mr Twinkle caught a bus and went right into the heart of the town. It was nice to be out of the rain. It had stopped when he got out and went around looking for a place to sleep. He found a tiny little room in a tall house, for which he would have to pay a shilling. Then he bought himself a loaf of bread, a meat pie, some cheese and butter and two apples. Aha – what a feast! He stored them all in his little room and then went out to find a job.

But nobody wanted him. Nobody at all. All he had ever done was to work at Mr Biscuit the Baker's. Mr Twinkle went back to his little room feeling very sad. Still, he cheered up when he set out his supper.

'It's such a feast,
It makes me smile

And I'll be happy
For a while!'

He hummed as he cut the meat pie in half. He was so very, very hungry that he ate everything except one apple and half a loaf of bread. He saved those for his breakfast. He curled up in bed and fell asleep, hoping that in the morning he would find some work to do – though perhaps that magic purse would be full of money again.

But it wasn't. It was quite empty.

'No money there!
It's plain to see
The purse is empty
As can be!'

hummed Mr Twinkle sorrowfully. He ate his breakfast of bread and apple and then went to put on his green mackintosh again. He put his hands in the pockets but they were quite empty. He remembered that he ought to have a handkerchief there, and he felt about for it. Ah – perhaps it was in the breast pocket – yes, something was there. But it didn't feel like a hanky. It felt like a little notebook. How strange! Mr Twinkle had never had a notebook in his life!

He pulled out a tiny brown notebook and looked at it. It certainly wasn't his. He opened it. A name and address were written inside. 'Jinky Jumble, 8 Popple Street, Cheer-Up Town.'

Mr Twinkle was amazed. How could the notebook have got there? Then a truly dreadful thought came to him, and he looked carefully at the green mackintosh. *Was* it his? Had he taken someone else's from the pegs in that little teashop?

It *wasn't* his! There was a name sewn on the loop at the back. 'Jinky Jumble'. It belonged to Jinky, whoever he was, not to Mr Twinkle! And dear me, yes, it did seem much newer and better than Twinkle's – and a different green.

Twinkle sank down on the bed and groaned. That purse hadn't been magic. It was an ordinary purse of money belonging to someone else – and he had spent all the money in it! He might be sent to prison! He certainly couldn't give back any of the money.

'The first thing to do is to take the mackintosh to its owner, and confess that I've spent the money!' said Twinkle, too sad even to make a little song about it. 'I must go straight away.'

So he left the cosy little room and asked his way to 8 Popple Street. It wasn't very far away.

It was a shop – rather a nice little shop that sold homemade cakes and biscuits, and new loaves of bread, all brown and crusty. Over the shop was the name of the owner, 'JIMINY JUMBLE'.

He must be Jinky Jumble's father, thought Twinkle. *Oh, dear – I hope he won't be very fierce with me – and if he calls the police I really shall run for my life!*

He went into the shop, and stood there waiting, the green mackintosh over his arm. A plump woman with a cheerful face came into the shop from a room behind.

'What can I serve you with?' she asked.

'Please,' said Mr Twinkle, 'I've made a dreadful mistake. I took Jinky Jumble's mackintosh instead of mine from the little teashop yesterday. And I found a purse inside and because I thought the mackintosh was mine, I – er – well, I spent all the money!'

Just then a little man came into the shop too. It was Mr Jiminy Jumble. 'Ho!' he said. 'So you spent it, did you? Well, repay it! That's the thing to do. That's easy! My son Jinky came home in *your* old mackintosh – and very old it must be too, and only fitted him because you're so small. You just pay him the money you took out of his purse and we'll say nothing more about it.'

'It was very honest of him to come and own up,' said Mrs Jumble.

'Yes, it was – and it will be honester still if he pays up,' said her husband.

'I'd like to, but I can't,' said Mr Twinkle. 'I've no money at all, you see. But, if you'd let me, I'd come and work for you for nothing, and work well too. I've been in Mr Biscuit the baker's shop for years and years, so I'd find the work easy here. Let me come and I'll work till I've paid off the money!'

'Well, well – it's the only thing to do, I suppose,' said Mr Jumble. 'Can you start today?'

> '*This very minute*
> *I can start*
> *With willing hands*
> *And grateful heart!*'

sang Mr Twinkle gladly.

Mrs Jumble laughed. 'Why, you're quite a poet!' she said. 'We can do with someone to help us. Mr, er – Mr...'

'Twinkle,' said Twinkle with a little bow.

'Mr Twinkle,' repeated Mrs Jumble. 'We'll pay

you a pound a week, and as much food as you can eat – and you can sleep in the little room off the kitchen.'

'Fine, fine!' said Mr Twinkle. 'I shall be able to pay you what I took out of that purse before many days are over, and have something left to go out and find another job.'

Well, he didn't have to go and find another job. He was so honest and kind and hard-working that Mr Jumble wouldn't hear of him leaving at the end of the week. 'We like you, Twinkle!' he said. 'We can't let you go. You're the best worker I ever had, and my little Jinky is so fond of you that he'd cry his eyes out if you went. No – you stay with us!'

'Oh, Mr Jumble,
I will stay
And never, never
Go away!'

sang Twinkle in delight. And there he is still, weighing out biscuits, slicing cake, helping to bake the sweet-smelling bread – and humming his little songs a hundred times a day! And here's the little song he's singing now.

> '*When things are going*
> *From bad to worse,*
> *Perhaps you'll find*
> *A magic purse,*
> *And change your luck*
> *In such a way*
> *That every day's*
> *A happy day!*'

You won't find a magic purse – but I hope the last two lines come true for you!

Ripple Gets a Necklace

Ripple Gets a Necklace

RIPPLE WAS a water pixie. She lived in the Long Pond where the water lilies grew, and she was as pretty as a picture and as proud as a peacock. She swam in the pond all day long, talked to the big frogs, tickled the old fish, and teased the moorhens that came to nest there.

'You know, Ripple would be so nice if she wasn't so conceited,' said the water vole one day, as he sat nibbling a water plant. 'She's always showing off.'

'She cuts the water lily leaves to pieces, trying to make herself new dresses every week,' said the moorhen, pecking a bit of the vole's plant. 'Do you think it is safe to nest here this spring, water vole? Last year Ripple kept tipping my babies out of their nest whenever I swam off. It didn't really matter because they could swim as soon as they were hatched – but it made them so tired having to climb back a score of times a day.'

'Oh, Ripple doesn't care how she teases anyone,' said the vole. 'She tied a water beetle and a dragonfly grub together the other day, and they were so angry that they nearly ate each other! She's so vain that she thinks she can do anything.'

Now the next day Bufo, the large old toad who lived under a big stone on the bank of the pond, invited everyone in the pond to a party at his end. They were to come and have games and fun. Ripple was invited too, and she at once began to think what kind of dress she could make for herself.

'I shall be the prettiest person there,' she said. 'I'll have a new dress, and a new ribbon in my hair and a new necklace.'

Well, she cut up five lily leaves for a dress. The lilies were angry, for the leaves were new and a very pretty red colour underneath. But Ripple didn't care!

And then Ripple found some lovely long strands of white jelly-like stuff set with little black beads threaded in and out of the water plants. It was toadspawn, but she didn't know it. 'Just right for a necklace,' she cried. She unwound it carefully and then wound it round her own neck. There was enough to make six rows of black and white beads.

Ripple was delighted and very proud. She couldn't think why everyone laughed when they saw her!

The party day was the next day, very bright and warm and sunny. Ripple went along with everyone else to old Bufo, the toad. He frowned when he saw her and seemed very cross. But Ripple didn't care. She knew she looked beautiful in her new dress and necklace.

And then she felt something tickling her. Something wriggled down her front and something wriggled down her back! She screamed.

'What is it? There's something crawling all over me.'

And indeed there was – for the toadspawn necklace had hatched into tadpoles that had wriggled down her neck! There were dozens of them, little black things that tickled all the time.

'It serves you right,' said Bufo, with an expression like thunder. 'How dare you come to my party wearing a necklace of toad's eggs? Go home at once!'

Ripple didn't go home. She ran right away from that pond, for she was so ashamed of herself. So the moorhen has built her nest there once again, for now she knows that her nestlings will be safe!

Thirsty Weather

Thirsty Weather

I WANT you and Joan to look after the hens for me this week,' said Mother. 'Gardener is away ill so there is more to do. You, Ben and Joan can quite well feed the hens, give them fresh water and clean them out.'

'Oh, we'd love to!' said Ben joyfully. 'Looking after hens is fun, Mother.'

'It's also hard work, if you're going to do the job properly,' said Mother. 'Twice a day the hens must be fed, once a day given fresh water, and twice a week their house must be cleaned.'

'That's easy!' said Joan. 'I'll feed them, Ben, if you'll do the cleaning and the watering.'

Well, the children did the hens well on Monday. On Tuesday they did too. But on Wednesday it was a hot day and Ben was tired when he had cleaned out the henhouse, and didn't want to bother to fetch water for the drinking bowls. 'I'll do it later,' he said.

But of course he forgot – and when Mother went down the garden, there were the eight hens, all gathered gloomily together round the empty water bowl. Later on, Ben and Joan went to Mother. 'Oh, we're so hot,' said Ben. 'Can we have a drink of lemonade, Mother?'

'Joan can,' said Mother. 'But you forgot to fill the water bowls for the hens, Ben, and let them go thirsty. So now you must go thirsty yourself.'

Ben remembered the hens' water on Thursday and Friday – but he forgot again on Saturday! And when he and Joan begged for ice creams, Mother shook her head.

'Neither of you can have an ice cream,' she said. 'You, Ben, have forgotten the hens' drinking water again – and you, Joan, must have seen that the drinking bowl was empty, and yet you didn't remind Ben. The poor hens were so hot and thirsty when I went down the garden. Now you can go hot and thirsty too.'

'It's dreadful to be so thirsty,' said Ben to Joan, as they went into the garden. 'My tongue wants to hang out like a dog's. I know what the hens felt like now! I've been horrid to them. After all, we can go and get water from the tap. The hens can't. I'll never, never forget again, Joan.'

And he didn't – so that was a very good thing!

'What a Shock for Jeff!

'WILL YOU please bring back the book you borrowed from me last week, Jeff?' said Alan.

'Oh, sorry – haven't you had it back yet?' said Jeff. 'I'll bring it to school tomorrow.'

'Thanks,' said Alan. 'It's one of my best adventure books, and I want to read it again.'

'Right,' said Jeff, and off he went, whistling.

'You'll never get your book back,' said Eileen to Alan. 'He's got *three* of my books. I just *can't* get them back. And he's got a lovely horse book belonging to Jack too. He keeps saying he'll give them back but he never does. He's a terrible borrower.'

Eileen was right. Jeff didn't bring back Alan's book the next day as he had promised. He just laughed and said, 'Well, I'd too many school books to carry. I'll try and remember tomorrow.'

'What about that Famous Five book I lent you?' said Dick, coming up. 'I've got the whole set except that one – and you've had it a week. Surely you've read it by now!'

'I haven't *quite* finished it,' said Jeff. 'You shall have it on Saturday. I'll bring it round.'

But he didn't, of course. Dick was very angry. He didn't like to see his fine set of 'Fives' with a gap in the middle. He went round to Alan's house on Saturday afternoon to see if Jeff had given him back his adventure book.

'No. It's too bad,' said Alan. 'But what can we do about it? It's no good being nasty about the books – Jeff can be *twice* as nasty. He's much bigger than we are!'

'Well – let's *both* go round to his house together,'

said Alan. 'We'll be two to one then. I'll ask for my book and you can ask for yours. He'll only just have to go up to his bedroom and get them. I don't see how he can refuse the two of us.'

'All right. Let's go now,' said Dick. So the two boys went round to Jeff's house, and rang the bell. Jeff's mother came to the door, a kind-faced, worried-looking woman, who smiled at the two waiting boys.

'Did you want Jeff?' she said. 'He's out, I'm afraid.'

'Oh – well, we just came to ask him for two books we'd lent him,' said Alan. 'We want them back rather badly.'

'There now! Jeff's always borrowing books and not giving them back,' said Jeff's mother, vexed. 'I'm so sorry. Look, would you just pop up into his room, where his bookcase is – and find your own books? And if there are any there belonging to your friends, you'd better take those too, if you will. I'm *tired* of telling Jeff to return books he borrows.'

'Oh, thank you,' said Alan, pleased. 'I really would love to have my book back. Come on, Dick.'

The two boys went up the stairs and into Jeff's bedroom. He had quite a big bookcase there, full of books of all kinds. Dick saw his 'Five' book at once!

He pounced on it. 'Here's my book – *Five Go To Smuggler's Top*! Good. Now where's yours, Alan?'

Alan found his adventure book – and then the two boys saw Jack's lovely horse book on the top shelf. Dick took it out and looked inside. Yes, it had Jack's name in it.

'We'll take this back to Jack,' said Alan. 'He *will* be pleased. And look – isn't that circus book one of Eileen's? Let's look inside and see.'

'Yes, it *is* Eileen's!' said Dick indignantly. 'It's got her name *and* address in it! And here's another of hers – *Six Cousins at Mistletoe Farm*! Honestly, Jeff's more than a borrower – he's halfway to being a thief!'

'Sh!' said Alan. 'His mother will hear you.'

Oh, dear – Jeff's mother *had* heard! She was just

coming into the room when Dick spoke. She looked at him and he went red.

'Oh, Dick – what a dreadful thing to say!' she said. 'Surely Jeff hasn't kept books long enough to make people think he's going to keep them for himself?'

'Well – there's a book here that he borrowed last term from someone,' said Dick, longing to run downstairs and out of the house. 'Perhaps he's just . . . just careless, Mrs Hayes.'

'No. No, it's more than being just careless, to keep things so long,' said Mrs Hayes sadly. 'Look, Dick – take out every book and look inside to see if it has someone's name in it. If it has, take it, and please give it back, as I said. If Jeff won't do it, then someone must do it for him!'

'We'll have a quick look,' said Alan, and then he and Dick took out each book, and looked inside for the name of the owner. If it had someone else's name inside, not Jeff's, they put it on the floor – and good gracious me, how the pile grew! It was really astonishing.

'Why – he's hardly got *any* books of his own!' said Alan, amazed. 'How in the world are we going to take these away, Dick? We can't possibly carry them.'

'I'll fetch my garden barrow,' said Dick. 'Wait here for me. I won't be more than a few minutes. You finish looking at the bottom row of books.'

Dick ran downstairs and out of the house. He lived just round the corner, so it didn't take him long to fetch his garden barrow. It was quite a big one, which was lucky – for guess how many borrowed books there were to wheel away?

Thirty-seven! Goodness, what an amount! The boys carried them downstairs, and piled them into the barrow. Mrs Hayes came out to say goodbye. She was horrified when she saw so many!

'We're not taking a single book belonging to Jeff,' said Dick. 'These belong to me and Alan and Eileen and Jack and Nora and Tom – and to quite a lot of others. We'll return them to each owner on Monday.

I'm afraid Jeff's bookcase looks rather empty, Mrs Hayes. There's only about seven books left!'

'Oh, dear! Well, it's about time he had a shock,' said Mrs Hayes, looking very worried. 'Please don't lend him any more books!'

Jeff was most astonished when he came home that afternoon and went up to his bedroom. The first thing he saw was his almost empty bookcase! He stared at it indignantly.

'Mother!' he shouted down the stairs. 'Where have all my books gone?'

'Alan and Dick came for books you had borrowed,' said his mother. 'They took them away in a barrow.'

'*Well!* How *dare* they take my books?' cried Jeff. 'They've only left seven. I had many more than that!'

'Well, ask them about the books on Monday,' said his mother.

So, when Monday came, Jeff marched angrily to school. He stamped into the cloakroom, where the children gathered before going into school, taking off their coats and changing their shoes. He saw a little crowd round Dick and Alan and went up, red with anger.

He saw that Dick had his barrow there, full of books – books taken from Jeff's bookcase. Jeff recognised them at once. He gave a shout.

'What are you doing with my books? How dare you take them out of my bookcase?'

'They're not your books,' said Alan, picking them up one by one to read the names. 'Eileen – here's a book of yours – catch. Here, Jack – this is your horse book. Nora, isn't this yours? Yes – it's got your name in it. And here's another.'

'I tell you they're *my* books,' said Jeff. 'Stop giving them out like that!'

'All right – come and give them out yourself,' said Alan. 'Dick hand him the books one by one – he can certainly keep any that are his. Make him read the names inside.'

Jeff was caught then! He had to stand by the

barrow, take each book that Dick offered him, open it and see the name inside! He grew redder and redder, as he handed books silently to the owners. Then he suddenly flung a book down.

'You've played a mean trick on me! I won't look inside any more books! Do what you like with them!' And away he stamped, with angry, ashamed tears in his eyes!

'I don't think he'll borrow a book again in a hurry,' said Eileen, hugging all hers to her. 'Oh – I am glad to have these back again! Would you believe that anyone could borrow so many books and not give them back?'

'Oh, yes – heaps of people do that,' said Alan. 'My mother said some grown-ups do it. Perhaps we've stopped Jeff from growing into a borrowing grown-up. Wasn't he angry?'

'He was ashamed too,' said Nora. '*I* think he was crying! Don't let's tease him about it – unless he tries borrowing again!'

Soon everyone had their own books back, and the

barrow was empty. Dick wheeled it out into the playground just as the bell rang for Prayers.

I expect you'll want to know if Jeff ever borrowed a book again. Well, so far he hasn't. He hasn't even borrowed a rubber! But he's done something rather nice. He has saved up his money and bought two fine books for the school library.

'I bet his mother made him do that!' said Dick to Alan. 'They're jolly nice books. I'm borrowing one today!'

'Well, for goodness' sake *bring it back*!' said Alan with a grin. 'I'm a librarian, you know – and I don't want to have to fetch it back in a barrow!'

Look at My Doll

Look at My Doll

MARY HAD a very pretty doll called Belinda. She had curly golden hair, bright blue eyes and a little red mouth, just a bit open to show two rows of white teeth.

'You're lovely, Belinda,' Mary told her. 'And your clothes are beautiful too!'

So they were. Belinda wore a fine silk dress with a very full skirt, and a little white coat, short to the waist. She had a pretty hat trimmed with daisies and forget-me-nots, and a pair of red shoes and socks. So everyone said she was beautiful, and when Mary's friends came to tea they all wanted to play with Belinda.

'If only she could walk and talk!' Mary said a hundred times. 'But she can't. She just sits about and smiles and looks pretty. Belinda, couldn't you just stand up? I know you can't walk, but do try to stand.'

No, Belinda couldn't even stand. But she always smiled, no matter what happened to her. She could open and shut her eyes, and that pleased Mary, of course. But oh, if Belinda would only come alive!

Now, one very rainy afternoon, when the nursery was empty, somebody peeped in at the window. It was Look-About the elf. She often came to visit the toys, and they liked her.

'Hallo!' said the sailor doll, pleased to see Look-About's bright little face. 'Come in!'

Look-About came in. 'My word!' said the teddy bear. 'You're soaked right through! Why didn't you bring your umbrella?'

'I did,' said Look-About. 'I was on my way to tea with my aunt Cheery, and I had on my best clothes, and I took my umbrella in case it rained.'

'Well, it did rain,' said the sailor doll. 'What happened to your umbrella?'

Look-About's little face puckered up as if she was going to cry.

'You know that old goblin who lives in the pansy bed? Well, he was out too, and he had his new hat on. And when it began to rain, he was upset because he thought it might get spoilt. So, when he saw me coming along with my umbrella up, he ran at me, snatched my umbrella and went off with it before I could stop him.'

'The nasty, horrid thing!' said the teddy bear.

'So, of course, I got absolutely soaked,' said poor Look-About. 'A-tish-oo!'

'There! You're getting a cold already,' said the bear fussily. 'What can we do about it?'

'Nothing,' said Look-About. 'I simply must go to tea with Aunt Cheery. It's her birthday. So I must go off in my wet clothes, I'm afraid – and, oh, dear, it's still raining!'

'It will soon stop,' said the sailor doll, looking

out of the window. 'You ought to dry your clothes, Look-About.'

'I know what she can do,' said Belinda's soft little voice suddenly. 'She can wear my clothes! We can dry her clothes by the doll's house fire while she is gone, and when she comes back she can give me back my clothes and put hers on again, nice and dry.'

'What a good idea!' cried Look-About to Belinda. 'You are kind! I'm sure I should look lovely in your beautiful clothes, Belinda.'

Belinda took her clothes off and gave them to Look-About. The elf put them on carefully and, when she was dressed, all the toys crowded round her admiringly.

'Oh, you do look nice!' cried the bear.

'Yes, you really do,' said the sailor doll. 'Now it's stopped raining, Look-About. You can go safely away to your aunt's. Come back afterwards to give Belinda her clothes. We'll dry yours for you.'

'What's Belinda going to do without clothes

though?' suddenly asked the pink toy cat, coming out of his corner. 'Suppose Mary comes back and finds her undressed?'

'She's out to tea,' said Belinda. 'And, anyway, I shall just climb into my little bed and stay there till Look-About comes back.'

So, when Look-About flew merrily out of the window to go to see her aunt Cheery, Belinda, in her pink vest, got into her small bed. The sailor doll tucked her up. 'You're kind, Belinda,' he said. 'I like you.'

Now, Look-About's aunt Cheery was giving a party that day because it was her birthday, and it lasted rather a long time. So Look-About was late coming back. Everyone had liked her new frock, coat and hat, and she had had a very nice time indeed. She climbed in through the window of the nursery. 'I've had a lovely time,' she said. 'And I haven't spoilt your clothes at all, Belinda.'

'Shhhhh!' said the sailor doll, and pointed to the door.

'What's the matter?' asked Look-About. 'Why should I be quiet?' She ran across the floor to the cot where Belinda lay. And just at that very moment in walked Mary!

She saw Look-About running across the floor, and stopped in amazement. The elf had curly golden hair and blue eyes, just like Belinda, and, in Belinda's clothes, she looked exactly like her. Look-About was frightened when she saw Mary coming in. She didn't know what to do. She ran across the floor again.

'Look at my doll!' suddenly cried Mary. 'Oh, do look at my doll!'

Look-About tried to scramble up to the windowsill, but she fell down to the floor. She began to cry.

'I've hurt my knee!' she wailed in her high voice.

'My doll can talk!' cried Mary in delight. 'Belinda, come here! I never thought you could walk or talk.'

But Look-About didn't dare to go near Mary. She ran away again. 'Mother, Mother!' shouted Mary. 'Oh, do come and look at my doll!' All the toys sat still and watched except Belinda, who lay in her cot, her eyes shut. The sailor-doll could hardly stop himself from shouting to Look-About.

Mother didn't hear. Mary went to the open door and called loudly, 'Mother, do come and look at my doll. Mother, she's come alive!'

'I can't hear what you say, dear. Come and tell me!' called Mother's voice. Mary ran impatiently from the room to fetch her mother.

'Quick, quick!' cried the sailor doll at once. 'I'll get your clothes from the doll's house, Look-About. Belinda, help her undress.'

In a trice, the elf's clothes were taken from the doll's house, quite dry. Belinda leapt from her cot and began to undress Look-About quickly.

'Now dress quickly!' said the sailor doll, who was keeping an ear open for Mary and her mother. 'Oh, quick, quick!'

Belinda took all the clothes from Look-About and dressed quickly.

'They're coming, they're coming!' said the teddy bear, and he dragged Belinda to a corner. She sat down, flop, fully dressed. There she stayed quite still, following the rule of all toys that they must not move when humans are in the room.

Mary and her mother came in. 'There she is!' said Mary, pointing to Belinda. 'Belinda, run about again!'

But Belinda didn't move, of course. Mary's mother laughed. 'I thought it couldn't be true,' she said. 'You just imagined it all, dear!'

'Oh, I didn't, I didn't,' said poor Mary, almost in tears. 'Belinda, run to me and talk to me!'

No, Belinda didn't. It was terribly disappointing. Mother went out of the room, laughing. Mary picked Belinda up and began to undress her.

'It's your bedtime,' she said. 'Oh, Belinda, surely I didn't imagine it all? I did truly see you running about all over the nursery.'

She took off Belinda's coat, hat and dress. Then she stared in surprise at the little frilly petticoat.

'Why, Belinda!' she said. 'Where did this petticoat come from? It isn't yours! I've never seen it before. And look, it is marked with two letters in one corner – the letters L and A. What do they stand for? Belinda, you've got somebody else's petticoat on! Where did you get it?' Of course, Belinda didn't tell Mary. She guessed that when she changed clothes with Look-About in such a hurry she must have taken the elf's petticoat by mistake.

'There's something mysterious about all this,' said Mary firmly. 'Very, very mysterious. One day I shall find out all about it. Oh, yes, I shall, Belinda, and then I shall know how it was I saw you rushing about the nursery floor wearing somebody else's petticoat!'

Well, I expect Mary will find out now, because she is sure to read this story. Belinda still wears the petticoat with L.A. on it. And Look-About wears no petticoat at all, but she doesn't mind a bit.

What a peculiar thing to happen, wasn't it?

The Prize Rabbit

The Prize Rabbit

THERE WAS once a fellow called Mr Twinkle, and he kept a rabbit in an old hutch, much too small and not as clean as it should be. And one day, most surprisingly, his rabbit won a prize at a show. The prize was a big scent bottle, and Mr Twinkle took it proudly home to his wife.

His friends all came to see it, and looked at the rabbit too, in its old hutch.

'That rabbit will win you a lot of prizes, I shouldn't wonder,' said one friend. 'It's valuable now. You ought to buy it a nice hutch, or it might fall ill in that dirty old box you keep it in.'

'I'll go right away and get a hutch this minute!' said Mr Twinkle, feeling most excited at having brought home a scent bottle for his wife. 'Nothing is too good for my rabbit now!'

His friends went with him to a carpenter's, and Mr Twinkle looked at all the hutches there. He ordered a very fine one, and told the man to send it and the bill by the next day.

'That's a beautiful hutch you've chosen,' said his friends, and Mr Twinkle beamed all over his face. 'Now what about ordering a bag of good hay for bedding and some really good rabbit food. A rabbit like that ought to feed on the best of everything!'

So Mr Twinkle ordered a bag of hay, some dry food and four good lettuces from the greengrocer.

'Why not have a little silver plate made with the rabbit's name on, to nail on the hutch!' said his friends. 'That would be very grand indeed.'

So Mr Twinkle ordered that from the silversmith and then went home, very pleased indeed, feeling quite sure that his rabbit would win many prizes and make him as rich as could be.

But, oh, dear me, when all the goods came the bills came with them – and poor Mr Twinkle *did* get a shock! Three shillings for the greengrocer! Seven shillings and sixpence for the silversmith! And fifteen shillings for the carpenter! Twenty-five shillings and sixpence altogether!

Mr Twinkle had two shillings in his pocket. His wife had three, but she wouldn't give him any of it. Instead she scolded him for being so extravagant. 'You'll have to sell something to pay those bills,' she said.

Poor Mr Twinkle! He had nothing to sell, for he was very poor. He sat and thought what to do, and at last he brightened up. Of course! He *had* got somethig to sell! He went to the old hutch, opened the door and took out his rabbit. Off he went to a man he knew, and sold his prize rabbit for twenty-five shillings and sixpence. Then back he came happily and paid all his bills.

'Aren't I clever!' he said to his wife. 'I've sold the rabbit and paid the bills!'

'*Clever!*' said his wife, looking at the useless hutch, the silver name plate and the food. 'No, you're more foolish than the rabbit! What are we going to do with that grand hutch now? You'd better go and live in it yourself, Mr Twinkle!'

Which One Would You Have Been?

ONCE UPON a time there were twins called Jack and Jenny, and they were four years old. They lived with their mother and father and Granny.

One day their mother had to go out for the day, and she left the twins with Granny.

'Now you must be good,' she said, 'and try to help Granny all you can. Remember that she has a bad leg and can't go upstairs easily, or walk far. So you must be her legs.'

So the twins ran here and there for Granny, and fetched her anything she wanted. They fetched her a bunch of flowers from the garden, and helped her to put them into a big bowl. Jenny fetched her hanky from upstairs and Jack ran to shut the front gate when someone had left it open.

'Now I'm going to write a letter,' said Granny, 'and I will ask the baker to post it for me. Will you watch for him, please?'

So the twins watched and watched, but the baker didn't come. Granny had forgotten that it wasn't the day he came with his new bread and currant buns.

'Oh, dear!' she said, when the twins told her that the baker hadn't been. 'This letter *must* be posted! I suppose I must try and get along to the postbox myself.'

'No, don't, Granny! You might fall and break your leg!' said Jack. 'Mummy said we mustn't let you go out.'

'Well – you're not big enough to put the letter into the pillarbox, are you?' said Granny, looking at him. 'It's the red pillarbox at the corner. Are you tall enough to reach?'

'Not yet,' said Jack. 'I try and try but I just can't.

It's a pity we don't grow faster.'

'Well, Jenny is smaller than you, so she couldn't reach either,' said Granny. 'Oh, dear, oh, dear – why didn't I remember that the baker doesn't come today? This is a very, very important letter.'

She put it on the hall table. 'Well, Daddy will have to post it tomorrow when he goes to work,' she said. 'It must wait till then.'

The twins were sorry that Granny was upset about her letter. But it wasn't a bit of good trying to post it – Mummy always had to lift them up when they put letters into the big mouth of the postbox.

'Well, it can't be helped,' said Jack, and went out to play. But Jenny stood and looked at the letter. She remembered Granny's disappointed face. It must be dreadful to want to post a letter and not even be able to walk the little way to the postbox. What a pity she and Jack were so small!

She thought a little while longer. Then she remembered something! When she and Jack wanted to get anything from the top of the high bookshelf, they took a little stool and stood on it. Why couldn't she take the stool to the postbox and stand on that?

I can, I can! thought Jenny. *Oh, what a good idea! Why didn't I think of it before?*

She ran to get the stool, and then took the letter from the hall table. Off she went down the road to the red postbox, the stool under her arm. She set it down beside the postbox and stood on it. Ah, *now* she could reach the big mouth easily. She popped in the letter and heard it slither down inside. There – it was posted and Granny needn't be upset any more.

She picked up the stool and went back home again. Granny was in the hall, looking at the hall table.

'Where's my letter gone?' she said. 'And dear me, Jenny, what *are* you doing with that stool?'

'I went out to post your letter, Granny,' said Jenny, 'and I took the stool to stand on. That's all! I can *always* post your letters now, can't I? I'm quite tall enough with the stool!'

'You good child!' said Granny. 'What an idea! Well, well, you're cleverer than any of us. Jack, come and hear this – and then tell me why *you* didn't think of it too!'

'I suppose I didn't think hard enough,' said Jack. 'And Jenny did.'

That was just it, of course! And now, do tell me – which twin would *you* have been, the one who thought hard or the one who didn't?

Acknowledgements

All efforts have been made to seek necessary permissions.

The stories in this publication first appeared in the following publications:

'Eight Times Nine!' first appeared in *Enid Blyton's Magazine*, No. 21, Vol. 5, 1957.

'The Mouse in the Window' first appeared in *Enid Blyton's Magazine*, No. 10, Vol. 3, 1955.

'What! No Cheese?' first appeared in *Enid Blyton's Sunny Stories*, No. 189, 1940.

'The Two Boys' first appeared in *The Teachers World*, No. 1737, 1936.

'Sally's Stitch' first appeared in *Enid Blyton's Sunny Stories*, No. 292, 1943.

'The Brown Rat and the Wren' first appeared in *The Teachers World*, No. 1819, 1938.

'Keep Your Eyes Open!' first appeared in *The Teachers World*, No. 1829, 1938.

'Up the Chimney!' first appeared in *Enid Blyton's Magazine*, No. 23, Vol. 2, 1954.

'The Wishing Feather' first appeared in *Enid Blyton's Sunny Stories*, No. 405, 1947.

'Who Has Won?' first appeared in *Enid Blyton's Magazine*, No. 21, Vol. 3, 1955.

'The Boy Next Door' first appeared in *Sunny Stories for Little Folks*, No. 224, 1935.

'Bicycle Magic' first appeared in *Enid Blyton's Sunny Stories*, No. 386, 1946.

'The Kind Little Girl' first appeared as 'The Kind Little Girl Fed The Hungry Sparrows' in *Sunday Mail*, No. 1891, 1944.

'Harry's Fine Idea' first appeared in *Enid Blyton's Magazine*, No. 22, Vol. 5, 1957.

'The Little Girl Who Was Shy' first appeared in *Enid Blyton's Sunny Stories*, No. 262, 1942.

'The Biggest Piece of Luck' first appeared in *Enid Blyton's Magazine*, No. 20, Vol. 3, 1955.

'Annie Gets Into Trouble' first appeared in *Enid Blyton's Magazine*, No. 18, Vol. 5, 1957.

'A Pair of Blue Trousers' first appeared in *The Teachers World*, No. 1732, 1936.

'Eggs and Marbles' first appeared in *Enid Blyton's Sunny Stories*, No. 305, 1943.

'A Dreadful Mistake' first appeared in *Enid Blyton's Magazine*, No. 19, Vol. 5, 1957.

'Funny-One's Present' first appeared in *Enid Blyton's Sunny Stories*, No. 391, 1946.

'Donald's Trees' first appeared in *The Teachers World*, No. 1854, 1938.

'One Saturday Morning' first appeared in *Enid Blyton's Magazine*, No. 22, Vol. 5, 1957.

'The Boy Who Didn't Believe' first appeared in *Merry Moments Annual*, published by George Newnes in 1923.

'A Real Bit of Luck!' first appeared in *Enid Blyton's Magazine*, No. 5, Vol. 7, 1959.

'How Very Odd!' first appeared in *Enid Blyton's Magazine*, No. 24, Vol. 3, 1955.

'Ripple Gets a Necklace' first appeared in *The Teachers World*, No. 1869, 1939.

'Thirsty Weather' first appeared as 'Tit For Tat' in *Good Housekeeping*, Vol. 51, No. 4, 1947.

'What a Shock for Jeff!' first appeared in *Enid Blyton's Magazine*, No. 23, Vol. 5, 1957.

'Look at My Doll' first appeared in *Enid Blyton's Sunny Stories*, No. 408, 1947.

'The Prize Rabbit' first appeared in *The Teachers World*, No. 1673, 1936.

'Which One Would You Have Been?' first appeared in *Enid Blyton's Magazine*, No. 25, Vol. 5, 1957.